Unwashed Shorts

An Absurd Assemblage of
Tall Tales, Short Stories,
Odd Odes, and Total Tosh

Slapped together by
Richard Williams (Alias BuzzzWyrd)

Acknowledgements

Nobody really – did it all myself, including the drawings, but –

About half of these stories were generated from writing prompts given at the Bridgetown writers club which morphed into the South Wexford writers club operating out of Red Books in Wexford town. I thank the late great Denis Collins, the almost on time Michael Duggan, and the ever present Wally O'Neill (at Red Books) for their words of encouragement.
I should also thank my wife, Mary, for her forbearance.
I also thank the Civil Service for the inspiration to start writing, to stave off brain death.
Finally a small mention to the awesome Mick Roche, and Mighty James "The Buzzz" McIntyre, for not pleading with me to stop writing.
Oh, and thanks to Michael Duggan for the picture of me spouting some tripe at Juke's open mic in Wexford in a year BC (Before Covid-19)

Forward

A wise man once said "If you want to stay sane – go mad" or was it "If you want to go mad – trying staying sane"
I should know – I think it was me said it, but then I was always in two minds...

Anyway...

Why Unwashed Shorts as a title you wonder?

Well, no one but myself has edited this work.

Having never passed an English exam, despite it being my only language (apart from a plethora of computer programming languages) , things like proper grammar, apostrophises and spelling, are a near mystery to me. I make no apologies for any 'mistakes' contained herein.
Also – no one has censored the stories as to bad taste, or being non-PC.
So they come to you without any laundry work done, and no hand sanitisations were performed during its manufacture, thou rumour has it I might have worn a mask (Just to hide the truth).

And the Cover?

Sex sells I'm told, so why a loose approximation to myself in my birthday suit on the front...and back... Well, I couldn't get anyone else pose for me.

Oh! I should mention *I Tell You No Lie'* and *'Begrudgery'* were previously published in the South Wexford Writers Group first compilation book 'Some Write with Glue'. Also I think an audio reading of *'If Only'* by myself might be broadcast as part of a Spoken Word hour on Wexford's New Peoples Movement Radio. I believe it may also be included (not audio) in the first issue of the Wexford Bohemian which is due out August 2020.

Warning:
    May contain nuts, nudity, and bad grammar. Definitely contains implied sexual activity with no mention of precautions, bad language, crap drawings, an Exel Spreadsheet, multiple deaths, and comeuppances, consumption of alcohol (me – during the writing process) violence (not me) and a grumpy old man (maybe me)..

Contents

Sorted 8

"Water" 18

"Why ME" 24

Where's My Bleeding Luggage 44

The End of The World... 52

The Pact 60

Desire 84

"Nasty WeatherWe're Having" 86

I Tell You No Lie! 94

The Torturers Lair 104

Time on His Hands 108

Good v Evil..118

You Can't Ask for Coffee...130

"Shush" 132

There Ain't No Bleedin' Justice 136

Words I should Have Said 154

Do You Love Me? 158

Midnight, on the Dot..170

Begrudgery 208

If Only...212

Sorted

Sorted

"Sorted" said Slippery Steve as he sat facing his long term fellow felon, Dodgy Dave. Their job demarcations laid down, proceeds split agreed, discussion over.

'Sorted' Steve thought to himself *'you're doomed Dodgy. Serves you right you ugly bastard, nobody muscles in on my job. I don't share nothing. Everybody knows that'.*

That thought gave him pause.

He had been surprised that Dodgy had even agreed to meet before the job, and alone... OK it was neutral territory, and both of them turning up to grab the stones would have been disastrous. The job was easy, but any complication, and could be curtains for both of them.

He didn't ponder long, *'too late to worry about that now, cause it's Sorted."*

"Time to go Dodgy, thanks for the coffee" he tried to say, but he felt strange. He knew his mind said the words, but he didn't hear himself say them. Odd! He tried to stand up, but nothing happened, his legs refused to act on command. He looked down to his nether regions; everything looked in order, hands on lap, legs still attached, no chains, weights, or manacles. He then tried to lift his head up, to look upon Dodgy's ugly mug for clues. But that didn't work either; he was now gazing at his naval, so to speak. Next, he tried his hands to see if they could lift his now

Sorted

very heavy head. But again, apart from a subtle twitch of one finger, nothing moved.

It dawned on him that something was dreadfully wrong. His brain was drowning in treacle; the speed of his thoughts would lose a race with a dead snail. He wasn't sure where he was, or what he was doing. He struggled to remember what had got him here. *'Meeting, Dodgy's ugly face, rank breath, garlic, Dodgy ate loads of garlic, afraid of vampires, he's gon'a put a stake though my heart....'*

He struggled to regain control of his thoughts, *'Coffee, bastard brought coffee's, drugged ... bastard, I'll get you'*. The last bit was meant to be spoken aloud, but he knew nothing came out.

He concentrated on his hands, maybe he can get them up to strangle Dodgy, but he couldn't move a muscle. His thoughts fell back to the impending job, how did Dodgy know about it? It cost him dearly to get the Info from that idiot, Lonesome Lenny. He had to bribe him to go sick for the day, from his security guard job, *'Dearly'* did he say – well no! Not really, the dumb arse settled on Steve's wedding band as the down payment, and he'd never really cared about that ring. It was gold, and chunky, but Lonesome seemed far too pleased with himself, little did he realise, that's all he was getting. *'Slippery Steve never repays his debts'*.

But, Dodgy turns up at the pool hall last night demanding...demanding, would you believe, to be in

Sorted

on the job, and he knew everything, how? Lonesome tell Dodgy too? Hardly likely, those two never got on, more likely kill each other than talk if they met.
Or is Dodgy shagging the missus, that stupid dumb blond can't keep her mouth shut, or her legs for that matter.

He reflected for a moment, he had guessed that some poor soul was pleasing her recently; perhaps smashing her nose in wasn't one of his best actions. That night, his dinner wasn't ready and waiting for him, when he staggered in drunk. She couldn't smell a thing from then on, and dinners, if he got them were just as likely to be burnt. But, even if she couldn't smell him, Dodgy was still as ugly as sin, he didn't remember blinding her as well. '*The bitch was probably doing it out of spite; anyway once this job is done I'm off, gon'a leave her in the dust, ha! Why did I even tell her, I'm getting soft, she's nagging again about paying bills, nag, nag, nag, so I blabbed about the big one, she's becomes all attentive, and lovey-dovey, and I fall for it, idiot.*' He thought.

Slippery had regained some level of control of his thoughts back, but the treacle was threatening to drown him again. Why am I still sitting here, has Dodgy left, can't see, can't hear him, the bastards going to get the stones, hope he takes the wife as well. '*Shit, this is a fine pickle I've got myself into*' that last thought did not go anywhere near expressing the depth of his emotions right then, but at least it didn't burn a hole in the paper.

Sorted

How long before this wears off? He thought that would be a very important question, but was no longer quite sure why.

CRASH!

Something hit the floor; he felt it shock his whole system somehow. His vision had blurred, and he had a sensation of pain in his head. Slowly his eyes rebooted, focus drifted back to see a different view than before. No longer could he just see his hands in his lap, now his view was largely taken up by two big feet, encased in sandals! The sensation of smell broke through, temporarily melting the treacle in his brain. Those were Dodgy's infamously stinking feet, diseased toes poking out of holey once white socks. *'What the fuck'*, was Slippery's first thought, second, and third thoughts, until the shock of being in close proximity to such a stench shrivelled his nasal hairs, and shut down the receptors, and half of his already molasses-ed brain in protest. Or had he stopped breathing?

Gradually, the rest of the vista facing him started to register on his consciousness. One lone ant effortlessly walked up the wall Slippery's head now propped up against. That same wall had both of Dodgy's feet planted firmly upon it. Clouds of dust moats hovering, and coalescing to be attracted to stick to the wall. *No! hang on, It's the floor. The bastards pushed me to the floor. Or did I fall, that crash must have been me.*

Sorted

"For fuck sake Dodgy, if you're doing anything, then do it, get it over with" he thought, then quickly regretted it, thinking maybe it'll wear off quick. He still had a nagging feeling reaching out from the fog at the back of his mind that it better wear off quick. He was missing something important, something that he should remember, but the morass of his grey matter had swallowed it up again. He had a reason to move that was nothing to do with Dodgy smashing his brains in.

He had to stay conscious, had to get out, something he needed to do.
Another crash, like an earthquake broke his mental struggles, and his view changed again. It took a while for the dust to settle, clearing the view. He could no longer sense the presence of Dodgy's dodgy feet, but a new pungent and rank aroma assailed his nostrils, that seemed familiar. *Shit*, he thought, *Dodgy's sat me up again and he's pushing his ugly mug into mine. What's he doing now, is he going to tell me my fate, gloat and laugh in my face*. Steve's mind raced, as a snail would. He tried to spit, but once more nothing worked.

But Dodgy Dave didn't laugh, nor did he speak, just grinned stupidly. It occurred to Steve that Dave's head, like his, was also in contact with the floor, just like his. *What the fuck is he playing at*. The molasses in his brain stirred a little, and a thought aided by a fragment of memory prompted him to laugh himself. Steve remembered the drug loaded doughnuts he had brought, knowing Dodgy's inability to resist sugar

Sorted

coated treats, so Dodgy must have eaten them, as he had drunk Dodgy's laced coffee. For a short while he found the situation hilarious, wanted to slap Dodgy back and laugh with him at their own stupidity, but not for long. Then he wanted to smack Dodgy so hard he'd be even uglier than now, and would have cried if he could. Now he knew when both of them recover there will trouble. What if Dodgy rises first, he'd probably find a metal bar and smash his head in, there will be no pretence of a deal now. No, he had to recover first, and make sure Dodgy doesn't trick him again.

He managed to take in a bit more of his limited view and could see plenty of weapons to 'defend' himself with. He redoubled his efforts to get some movement or feeling back, maybe that will force the drug through his system faster.

He re-focused on Dodgy's face, to see if he had signs of movement. He himself had managed to move his eyes a bit, what of his rival. Dodgy's eyes were still staring fixedly ahead, straight into Steve's, he could almost feel the white-hot intensity of hate trying to burn holes through the back of his eye sockets. But to his relief, there was no movement, and was that a touch of desperation in those eyes.

Now, he felt he had the edge, a new hope swept through him, he tried even harder to move, with little or no effect. He tried to think, he had drunk coffee, a liquid, faster acting, got through to his nervous system faster, Dodgy ate doughnuts, a solid sticky mess, with

Sorted

enough drug in them to stop a rhino, takes longer to act and clear the system, Yes, he would win, and Dodgy knows it. He felt a slight movement of his lips, he managed a subtle smirk, and Dodgy's eyes could see it, Ha.

Other thoughts were struggling for his attention, he'd had a plan, what had it been. Something urgent, important, was hidden from him, niggling, annoying, requiring attention. He needed to be up and away, but why, what was it.

His field of vision increased slowly, so that his eyes came to rest on a nearby concrete pillar. He could see something strapped to it. It seemed important. He concentrated; it was some sort of contraption with wires, and a sort of digital clock with red figures constantly changing. He struggled to think through the fog, that device he knew it would be there, but why? The figures, numbers, counting down, it had just dropped below three figures. It was the reason he'd thought of this place, derelict building, in the basement, he looked at Dodgy again, his eyes were wide with terror.

Demolition, this place was to be demolished today, that's it, today at midday, in, in 5 seconds.

"Bugger"!

BOOOOOMMMM.

Sorted

The gathered crowd, watching from a safe distance waited. It looked as if nothing was going to happen. As if in slow motion, the whole building collapsed, straight down. A total success, and the crowd cheered, the most enthusiastic response came from a nasally challenged blond who wasn't as dumb as some halfwits thought. *"Well, that went well"* she said to herself, as she turned and retraced her steps back to the dingy flat she had shared with that bastard Steve. She was pleased with herself, telling Lonesome to talk to Steve and Dodgy about the job, telling Steve about the demolition job she was going to watch today, then "accidently" bumping into Dodgy before their meeting, and slipping the drug into both coffees, to be sure. She had already put the idea of the doughnuts into Steve's thick skull earlier.

Back in the flat, she finished her packing, zipped up the bags, and sat and waited. Not long after her new lover walked through the open doorway.

"How'd it go, Jane?" he asked.

"Well" she smiled, "and you, Lonesome?"

"Very well" he replied, "no hiccups, I reckon we've got days before the loot is missed, just need to take a pee".

"Good, give me the car keys and I'll load my bags, Oh! And help yourself to the doughnuts on side, be a shame to waste them".

"Water"

"Water"

"Water"

"Wha..." was the incoherent mumble that escaped from John's sleep drugged mouth.

"Water" was repeated by a gruff voice.

Johns muddled mind had no idea whether this was a statement, a request, or, for that matter, a dream.

"Water... wants drink" there it was again.

His mind couldn't work out the significance of the new information. He really wished that whatever reality this came from, it would leave him alone in his alcoholic stupor.

"ga.way" he pleaded into the pillow.

"Thirsty, need drink" the gruff voice had come closer to his exposed ear. The voice had gained an edge of urgency, demanding attention, and dampening his ear with a spray. John brought a free hand up to his ear, to find a damp stickiness.

He struggled to a sitting position, which caused his head to hurt, but kept his eyes clamped shut. The brightness of the morning light would be too much for him to bear at this moment. He tried to remember...

"Water"

What was it he was trying to remember... He couldn't think, mind stuck in neutral.

"Still need water" Now there was a pleading in the voice. "Thirsty" it added.

"OK, OK... hang on a minute, keep your knickers on" He blurted, to give time to regain some sort of limb control, and sense of balance.

"What knickers" came the response?

'Ah!' thought John, mind doing somersaults, what the hell did he get into bed with last night. *'If that's a girl with that voice...I'm in trouble...NO...IM' IN TROUBLE!'* Some fleeting memory of his miserable lonely evening, and night flashed through his head, painfully. He had been drinking alone, he thought. The voice is surely a bloke, surely not. Could he have been that drunk, was he that desperate?

"Love you" the voice spoke sincerely.

"Arg.." No...No...This can't be happening he thought. Nothing for it.... going to have to turn on the external sensors - that is – open his eyes to this bright new world he'd woken up into. He had to ignore the pain, and face the music.

"Water"

The shock of blinding light was worse than he feared. The pain lanced through his brain as he looked out of the two slits to see a dark shape before him. Once his eyes had managed to gain some focus the only living thing he could see was his dog's big soppy face staring back at him. No two-legged well endowed human of any persuasion could be spied anywhere in the room. Just big soppy Jasper, his only loyal friend, sitting expectantly before him. A surge of relief filled him, but only for a few seconds, before some sense of logic and reality burst back in to his mind. Jasper talking?

"What...That's it" he said to the room, lying back down and shutting his eyes "I'm never going to drink again – I'm on the wagon"

"All very well, but bowls still empty"

John's mind went into a panic. *'Fill bowl...voice goes away...yes'* He struggled to rise, keeping his eyes off of Jasper. He staggered his way out of the bed room, into the kitchen. *'Pick up Bowl... fill bowl...put bowl down...collapse'*. The first two commands he completed moderately successfully, but that last pair got confused. It was all too much. Over he went, head hitting off a table leg, and out went the lights again...

"Water"

Consciousness comes back slowly to John. *'Oh, what a weird dream I had'* Jasper was licking his face. Normality had returned, and so had the pain. *'I really must stop this drinking'*. At that point he had thought he had fallen asleep on the kitchen floor. *'This is bad'* he thought, *'too drunk to make it to bed, and dreaming of talking dogs'*.

"Stop licking Jasper" he said "Oh boy Jasper, never again... Ah, Love you boy".

"Love you too, but please fill my bowl before you drunk again, master!"

"Why ME"

"Why Me"

"Why Me?" the teenage boy asked petulantly.

"Because!" His father was not in the mood for this.

"It's not fair! Why me?" The lad was not about to give up.

"Look son, it's for your own good... And the good of the village" The father didn't sound too convincing.

"Mum doesn't agree".

"Your mothers a mother, they never agree, anyway she had her chance to change things"

"What do you mean Father...Change things?"

"Never you mind, now get ready"

"It's not fair, don't I get a say in this?"

"No, you don't, discussions over, now get dressed"

"In THAT!"

"YES, IN THAT"

"I'll look ridiculous"

The father sighed. "NO...YOU...WON'T"

"YES, I WILL, it's for girls"

"Why Me"

"No it's not, it's traditional"

"For Girls"

"NO it's NOT"

"When have you ever seen a boy wearing it?"

"What...Oh...Em... Your Uncle Eli, yes he wore it... Once."

"That was in a play... and anyway, he's a cross dresser, and a bit funny... you know"

"Don't you talk about your Uncle like that, he...he was a talented artiste. Nobody laughed at him"

"Yeh. They were too frightened he'd come up behind, and give them a surprise"

"I'll listen to no more of your insolence, get dressed...NOW"

"NO"

"What?"

"I refuse"

"YOU CAN'T refuse"

"WHY?"

"Why Me"

"Because!"

The father raised his hand as if to strike the boy down, but then thought better of it. The young lad had shot up in the last year, and was now taller than he was, and anyway, bruises wouldn't look so good. So he changed his approach.

"Look Son, it's a real honour to be chosen, think of your family, your Mother. If you don't go through with this, none of us will able to walk through the village again, without the shame, the shame of letting everybody down. You don't want that do you? And, before you ask, there's nobody else, you're it. So please, for your family, your friends, your....self respect, you'll be banished... or worse if you don't."

The two protagonists fell silent for a moment. The ground shuddered slightly, and outside Big Fella rumbled a complaint. The Island's dominant volcano was showing it's anger, which was the reason why the High Priest had made the call (according to the High Priest).

"Will it hurt?" the boy didn't look quite so defiant now.

"What..Oh...Nooo..." The father caught off guard, didn't seem too sure.

"It is going to hurt isn't it?"

"Why Me"

"No...Not if it's done right"

"It must hurt... The blade..?"

"Very sharp. Very quick, straight through. Won't feel a thing" The father appeared to be remembering something different.

"But Why me, why am I the only one to qualify"

The father clenched his fists, swore under his breath. "Cause you're a virgin... boy"

"But why only me?"

"CAUSE YOU'RE THE ONLY ONE...boy"

"What, you're joking – last week I thought there were many".

"Well that was before the High Priest's decree, and before that bloody missionary started saving girls souls, and mothers protected their sons" he spat with disgust, and pointed up at the rumbling volcano. The ground trembled again, and Big Fella spoke of its displeasure.

"See, now get dressed"

"But Father, what exactly is a virgin?" The young lad was acting dim.

"Why Me"

"What?... Oh come now, surely you're not that dim?"

"Please Father, what is it? Exactly"

"Oh, OK. It's someone who's never had sex"

The lad gave him a look that demanded further explanation, causing the Father some discomfort.

"Oh, god! For a girl...it's who hasn't been deflowered...A boy who hasn't deflowered a girl".

"They both have to be virgins for the boy to lose his?"

"No, No, No, Oh and boy on boy action don't count, so the priest says"

"Deflowered, take a flower from a girl? Jilly gave me one of her flowers she picked last week!"

"No...No.. it's not a real flower you idiot... Look OK right when a boy ... man puts his manhood, you know the dangly bit between your legs, and shoves it up a girls private parts" the boy maintained his dumb look, inwardly enjoying the man's squirming. "You know, between her legs" the boy raised his eye lids "Towards the front, not the back, that doesn't count either... Oh what am I saying – how would you know anyway"

"Oh – you mean Fucked then, cock up the cunt, like, then, why didn't you say so"

"Why Me"

"You!...OK fucked then, now you understand" Father cursed the boy, deep down, and thought '*what a blessing it will be to be shot of this one*'.

"Well, yes, but how does that make ME a virgin "

"Cause you've never done it, you stupid boy, God give me strength"

"But I have"

A short silence followed, the fathers expression slowly changed from exasperated through to startled

"You what?"

"I HAVE done it"

"What, with whom, and animals don't count... you spend far too much time with those goats of yours, seen you talking to them. You're far too friendly with those creatures, everybody says, it's embarrassing; George...The High Priest says you must be perverted. I've heard the whispering behind my back. To tell you the truth, I'll be relieved when this is all over. It's bloody embarrassing. "

"No Father I would never ever treat the animals like that. I would never do such a thing, I'm not like the High Priest ... and you."

"Why Me"

"What do you mean boy?"

"I did it with some else Father"

"No, no the High Priest abuses animals you saying, that's blasphemy, son, zip your lips boy, or you'll be in big trouble."

"I think I already am in as big a trouble as I could get, being sacrificed and all"

"That's an honour son; calling out the High Priest is a death sentence."

"What's the difference Father?"

"The difference? The difference is that I could still walk around the village, my head held high, with pride that my son saved the village from Big Fella's wroth.. That's the difference" The Father had a dreamy, self satisfied look on his face for a while, until he remembered the current argument.

"You better not have been spreading this filth around the village boy"

"No point Father, all the boys know, many of us have seen it with our own eyes, some of the girls know too."

"I don't want to hear any more, put on the dress at once"

"Why Me"

"Father – I told you I am not a virgin"

"Oh what now?. So tell me? Who was the unlucky girl then, the girls of the village avoid you, cause of the smell, and I never introduced you to the ladies of the night, and your sister would beat you up if you even touched her. Your brother wouldn't bother his arse helping you get laid, so who could you have possibly done the dirty deed with?"

"Mum"

"Mum what?" The Father stood hands on hips, head thrust forward, in a stance meant to be threatening, but the lad was defiant.

"Mum... It was Mum"

The pregnant silence that followed nearly reached maturity, before the pressure popped.

"What?" erupted the Father, weakly, spewing spittle at the boy?

"IT... WAS... Mother" he repeated slowly, and deliberately, to make sure the Father understood.

"Wha...When?" another attempted eruption petered out.

"Why Me"

"Ever since I showed her my first hard on, Mum taught me everything, you never taught me anything".

The Father wilted, and shrunk back, until a new resolution came back to his face.

"And she will back you up, will she?" if the Father had thought little of the boy before this moment, his feeling had now turned to hate. "She will own up to having SEX..." He spat the word with undisguised disgust before continuing "with... with her own son, Will she? Will she admit that that lump she's currently carrying is yours.. BOY" a hot stream of molten saliva ran from his mouth. "Shaming me, her dutiful husband, making out that my attentions were never enough...BOY?" He once again tried to adopt dominant stance, but suddenly realizing that his Son had out grown him, and now the lad stood tall and proud.

"Well... YOU NEVER ACTUALLY DID, did you, FATHER?" The man was taken aback by the venom with which the boy spoke. "She had to go to others for 'attention' DIDN'T SHE Father. You prefer the attentions of the High Priest...DON'T you?"

"That's...That's a dam lie" he spluttered.

"Why Me"

"She told me you're NOT my Father, you can't be, and you're not my half siblings Father either. You've never managed it with a girl yourself, have you DAD?"

"You've no proof; no one will believe you, a dirty little goat lover".

"I told you 'Dad' the boys and me have been watching you, and we've seen you two together, making like a beast with two heads, DAD"

A look of sheer evil came over the older man's face. "No one will believe you; the elders don't listen to boys."

"So, you don't deny it, then?"

"Why should I, if you seen it, and soon you'll be dead. Then I'll deal with your mother. That woman disgusts me. Only got married to stop the chatter. Don't understand what all fuss is about, I let her have her sordid fun, as long as she was discreet."

"Are you owning up to animals as well 'DAD'. Did you know I knew, about the High Priest? Is this why you two resurrected the sacrifice idea? It's been many years since it was done, and it didn't do anything that time. Then you leaked the news to the village that the High Priest was thinking of sacrificing virgins, after you sent me up the mountain on a wild goats chase. So I

"Why Me"

was out of the way while the villagers raped all the virgins left...for their own good ah?"

"You seemed to have worked it all out, and there I was thinking you were an idiot. Still all this talk is too late for you, once you leave here with that mask strapped on, no one will understand a word you scream. Yes I wanted rid of you, Yes, I knew, and once this is over, your Mother will meet with a tragic accident now you've told me of her shame, I'll not have your son in my family. Ha."

"So now you're telling me you're planning my Mother's death as well"

"Of course I am...I've never touched a woman, they disgust me, me and George are lovers, we've had half your flock of goats, and we cooked up the sacrifice to get rid of you...Now I've said it, and this delightful discussion is over"

With that, the man produced a club from behind him. "You don't have to be conscious going out that door, just not bleeding too much. I'll call in the honour guard outside, say you fainted, all over come with the honour of it all. You never know you might be dead before the High Priest fucks up your execution." He lifted the club to make the blow.

"Why Me"

The hut door burst open, and in rushed two of the village elders, followed by the honour guards. "Put that club down John, we've heard it all, and the boy's Mother's confessed to us".

The man dropped the club, and a small snarl burst from his lips "So what's my crime Elder?

"Firstly, Defaming the High Priest, by claiming he only arranged the sacrifice to protect his position."

"It was the boy who claimed that, I was just leading him on"

"You confirmed it. Second, inferring that the High Priest performs bestiality"

"Same thing, it was the boy"

"Thirdly, presenting for sacrifice someone you believe to be a non-virgin"

"Hardly matters, he'll be executed for blasphemy anyway, you heard him"

"Fourthly, conspiracy to murder your wife"

"I was joking, to upset him, no proof"

"And finally and most importantly.

"Why Me"

Not owning up to your own virginity, and as the oldest virgin in the village, apart from the high priest, it was your duty to volunteer yourself for sacrifice."

"What? I was joking – you can't prove that"

"Your wife says otherwise, she told us how you hate women's bodies, and how you arranged for others to do your duty for you".

"So, she could be lying to save her bastard".

"Ah, you admit he is not yours. Oh and just to be sure I've questioned every woman in the village and all of them deny ever being with you."

"You can't prove that, they are all lying, the High Priest will never stand for this"

"You can't prove the opposite, and since the High Priest has demanded a sacrifice, and the ceremony is about to start, we have no time for further investigation. So you will prepare yourself for sacrifice."

"But you can't, you heard me, the whole things a set up to get rid of this nuisance, its irrelevant now"

"High Priests decree, it's the law. While he's still in office, it must be obeyed "

"He'll rescind it, I'm sure" he said without resolve.

"Why Me"

"Too late, the time is now. But the young lad can challenge the High Priest after you're gone"

"But he is not a virgin - you heard him - got to be a virgin to challenge, and there won't be another for years"

"Oh that. He was lying; we thought it the best way of getting the truth out of you, considering the lack of time. Anyway with the rumours about you and the priest spreading around the village, I think the lads a shoe in, after all, old George won't last forever, he's eighty now, we better get someone young in before it's too late"

With no further ado, John was grabbed, the dress pulled over him, mask thrust onto his head, cloak of feathers draped around his sagging shoulders, and he was marched by the honour guards, unceremoniously out the door and down the path to the sacrificial platform followed by one of the Elders.

"Thanks, Dad" said Tom looking straight at Thomas the Elder. A look of embarrassment passed across Thomas's face. "Don't you tell anyone... how did you know?"

"Mum told me we're named after our fathers, so I guessed"

"Why Me"

"Well done, but keep your trap shut and I'll see you get the High Priests position, you can't be any worse than old George"

Tom's mother entered the hut, and hugged her son, and then sent him to check on the goats. Once he'd left the hut she turned to the Elder, "Thank you Thomas, thank you"

"Please don't call me by name, address me properly from now on, I don't want any suspicion falling my way, you understand?"

"Sorry... Elder. But it is all right. Your wife won't hear from me... along as Tom becomes High Priest..."

"There's still that Missionary"

"You really shouldn't have trusted Bernards confessional, my love. Still, nothing to worry about there, now, he hung himself this morning" she attempted to kiss Thomas on the lips. He shrunk back "How?"

"By his rosary beads, didn't put up a fight, too drunk really, and you've dealt with his devils' spawn, haven't you, dear?"

"Why Me"

"Of course, with pleasure, you know you're an evil woman Jezebel, that Missionary was right" He smiled and kissed her quickly, but with passion.

"I must go, must be seen at the ceremony, you and the boy better stay away. It wouldn't do for you two to be cheering too loudly"

With that he departed, and Tom came back in the back door.

The Mother and son watched the farce from the little house. They saw the high priest fall over, heard him forget his lines, and having to be prompted from the side by his assistant, a small boy with a sore bum. The 'victim' was forced onto the altar by the two strongest men of the village, muffled noise coming from behind the mask. The High Priest, who was clearly drunk, fumbled, and dropped the sacrificial knife while mumbling the words of the ceremony. Finally, he had to be helped to plunge the blade into the heart of the victim, as Big Fella had started to show a greater displeasure at the antics below him. At the point the sacrifice stopped struggling; Big Fella shuddered with disgust, spat rocks, and broke ground. The air was full of his wrath, and brimstone. It lasted but a minute, before he fell back to sleep and the air cleared enough to see again. On the high ceremonial platform, the lone figure of the small boy stood with a

"Why Me"

big grin on his face and his hand raised with a thumbs up towards Tom and his Mother. Down below him lay the twisted form of the, now former High Priest, with a clearly broken neck.

"Well, that went well" Jezebel reflected.

"Good boy, that Simon" added Tom "and it a nice touch from the Big Fella – don't tell me you got him on your side too Mother"

"No Tom, Bernard told me"

"What? Is his religion the right one then?"

"No dear, No...He told me he studied 'volcanoes', I think he called them, across all of the Islands before he ended up here. He was fascinated by them. I think he was going to use his knowledge to make himself king"

"Oh, so he had to die too?"

"Yes dear"

"And you didn't tell Thomas about us then?

"No dear, wouldn't have gone down too well, I wouldn't want to disappoint him. You see, he has to maintain that it is his wife that can't conceive, an infertile Elder is just not on, and he would lose status. So when

"Why Me"

you're high priest, you can decree that widows will be the ones sent to serve... hand...and foot...and elsewhere, dear...and he will enthusiastically adopt our child once born, and everyone will be let believe it was his in the first place, and be reassured that our Elders are fertile men, and everyone will be happy. His wife will be relieved – she was considering getting shagged by half the village, but she always preferred other women, if you know what I mean, and she was horrified at the thought of childbirth. If Thomas KNEW the child wasn't his – well it could spoil everything, dear"

"But I'm named after him! Surely I'm his?"

"Ssh dear, don't spoil things"

"Oh Mother, you think of everything, but what was that about your devil spawn...was that my half brother and sister".

"Brother and sister dear, Yes".

"Did Thomas make them disappear? Why?"

"No dear, they disappeared themselves".

"Why?"

"Virgins of course".

"Why Me"

"Pardon...I know Berna was ugly as sin, but she was as strong as two blokes, could have frightened the whole village into "saving" her. All the girls wanted to 'know' Bear, always preening himself, look at me I'm handsome strutting round the village. Why...?"

"Yes. Strange, I know, neither of them was your 'Fathers' yet they followed him in a few ways"

"Gay?"

"No dear, Goats, why do you think your animals took fright so much. My 'dear' husband sent them off together to hide in a cave, you know, one of those that Big Fella uses to spout lava when he's angry. I got Thomas to block the exit... Stupid that was the other trait of your... my ex-husband" she paused, and took his hand, and held it to her bump.

"You really have thought of everything, Mum" said Tom as his Mother led him off to the bedroom.

Big Fella stirred in his sleep, still annoyed with the antics of the parasites that infested his sides. Next time, he vowed I'm getting rid of the lot...Soon.

Where's My Bleeding Luggage?

The rain is pouring yet again
Like it will never ever stop
I'm looking out the window
As gutters overflow their top
At least the year's big tasks done
We got the Christmas shop
And we're going away for Xmas
To where there's rarely a drop

Yes. We're going away for Xmas
For the disparate family to unite
Up at an unearthly hour
Off to get a long haul flight
Loaded down with luggage
We're not travelling light
Off down the misty mountain
Into the sleepless night

Delays for fog in Gatwick
The announcer has us told
Delays for baggage errors
We sit on a plane getting old
Delays for fog again
As to the run way slowly rolled
Still another long, long, day
With no sleep yet to unfold

Finally land in Vegas
After a lifetime on the plane
Stiff, numb, and exhausted
Flight delays fried my brain
Got to the hall of baggage
Watched the carousel in vain
Round and round went cases
in my head was this refrain

>Where's our bleeding luggage
>Gone to god knows where
>Where's our bleeding luggage
>I think I'm going to swear

Standing at the carousel
Stumped at what to do
Fifteen times the same bags
Reappeared into my view
But none were like our stuff
As our anxiety grew
All the Christmas presents
Gone! So who can we sue?

We grabbed an airport worker
And pleaded for advice
"Oh you poor souls – got no luck"
We rolled with loaded dice
"Did you get insurance"
At least we paid the price
Then he gave us directions
And wished us a day that's nice

    Where's our bleeding luggage
    Gone to god knows where
    Where's our bleeding luggage
    I really I'm going to swear

We trudged off down to Recheck
But the queue was long and wide
With a crowd of other losers
For attention there we vied
"You've lost our bleeding luggage"
My wife politely cried
We'll have to go commando
"A sight to see", I lied

The lady took our details
As we told our tale of woe
Describing our suitcases
Tied up with a pink bow
How it contained presents
From Santa, Ho! Ho! Ho!
She sympathized with practice
But still she didn't know

    Where's our bleeding luggage
    Gone to god knows where
    Where's our bleeding luggage
    With all my underwear

We left the airport building
Feeling very down
Met by friendly faces
But we could only frown
"they lost our bleeding luggage"
As they drove us into town
At least we got the duty free
Our sorrows for to drown

Oh! Sweet joy and happiness
We finally got the call
They found our bleeding luggage
They left in the baggage hall
They'll deliver it tomorrow
No need for the shopping mall
The kids will get presents
Oh sweet joy they'll have a ball

    We're getting our bleeding luggage
    Only 3 days late
    We're getting our bleeding luggage
    Not long now to wait

The dessert rain is pouring
First time here for years
Still ain't got our luggage
The wife's in floods of tears
It arrived in the airport
4 days ago one hears
So we're off to Wallmart
To get in some Christmas Cheers

    Oh! Give us our bleeding luggage
    Already 6 days late
    We ain't got our luggage
    Full of melted Chocolate

T'was on the seventh day
As the desert sun was setting
Door bell ring announced
Our luggage we are getting
"Thank god" our hosts declared
"It truly is a blessing"
No – Fedex and our luggage
 At least that what I was betting

    It was our bleeding luggage
    Hip hip hip hooray
    It was our battered luggage
    I've nothing left to say

The End of The World...
As we know it

The End of The World

Honest Jim sat behind his betting shop counter cursing his luck. Worst day for years he thought. No need to hide anything from the tax man today. Not much time left before the last race of the day and little other sport of interest this evening.

He gazed out into the public area at his remaining customers. Half a dozen, or so, stragglers were still in the shop. Gave him some hope of regaining part of the day's losses. Luck is usually no friend to this bunch of losers. Jim held this lot in deep contempt. It appalled him to think that this dross was his bread and butter, but at the same time it gave a warm feeling inside to know that they depended on his services to keep what was left of their sanities, and hopes, alive. "Fools" he thought as a small lopsided smile crept across his face.

His thoughts were cut short by the hesitant opening of the front door. It caused a few of the less absorbed heads to turn, those that were not glued to their desperate hopes. There was a sharp intake of breath from the swivelling heads as the new entrant came partially into view. In the poorly lit doorway was a shape and form to terrify the poor inmates of this establishment. Its colour was pure black. Not of skin, although very little of that was visible. On saying that,

The End of The World

more skin, face wise, was exposed than had it have been a stereotype Muslim female suicide bomber. Even so, to the punters within, this was the most horrifying visitation possible, ignoring the arrival of a wife, or mother, come to pull the poor soul back to their home by the ear.

In the shadowy entrance there stood the form of an occupied Nuns habit. The punters plunged their hands into their pockets to protect their small change. A collection box and a cull of guilty consciences were bound to appear next. But the shadow did not speak, implore, accuse, or ask for anything. No box, or leaflet materialised. The shape just stood mirroring the disconcerted looks of the inmates. All on the public side of the counter were way outside their comfort zones.

On the other hand, behind his counter, Jim just thought "That's all I need right now". Already a couple of the guilty had run out the back door , something about "time for a fag". "*There's a few quid I won't get back to day*". He resolved to get rid of this apparition proto, before more customers remember that they believe in god, and take their winnings home to their "loved" ones.

The End of The World

"This is a betting shop, sister, the Salvation Army's next door, easy mistake" he chimed.

"Oh!, right" it spoke, and moved a step further into the light. Any reassuring thoughts that it was probably that joker Andy in his party gear just trying to scare the wits out of his fellow punters, evaporated. Though why anybody would have thought that since the man himself was one of the terrified punters present. Hopes of this not being a genuine sister of whatever was dispelled by the sight of an angelic face that could only belong to the pure hearted, according to those who had lost the souls in a bet.

The vision took another hesitant step forward.

"I...I know, em, can... can I place a bet, please" the vision of heaven asked non too confidently.

Now Jim was way out of his comfort zone. "Arg" was his comeback, until his natural ingrained greed, and his joy of stealing sweets from babies kicked in. "Well, yes, right, come up to the counter Sister, what can we DO you for" he spoke honestly for once. At no point did he think – this is wrong.

She glided forward, serenely, to the counter and beckoned Jim to lean close so she could whisper. Jim obliged, he was intrigued, and a little bit excited to be

The End of The World

so close to such pure beauty."What do you want to bet on, Sister" he oozed.

"The End of the World"

"What?

"I said the end of the world, at quarter to six, this very day" The vision replied just loud enough for every straining ear to hear.

"Arh...What" Jim was lost.

"The end of the world, at quarter to six, this very day" she said with more intent.

"What...em, but why do you think that's even a possibility"

"I had a vision, saw it clear as day, God told me" Now she was defiant

While Jim was still trying to get his head above water, she added " What odds would you give on that"

"Oh... I..em...Oh..million to one" he offered, while deep inside he felt a warm feeling he always felt when he considered himself being mean with the odds.

The End of The World

The Nun nodded at that, and slapped a wad of notes on the counter "I'll take those odds, here's five hundred, and I want proof of the bet".

Well thought Jim, this days looking up, this stupid bitch will put this day back into the "black". He laughed internally at his little private joke, as he wrote out the betting slip. It occurred to him to ask her how the "hell", ha ha, did she expect to collect her winnings after the end of the world, but didn't want to risk her regaining her senses and taking back the dosh, so he just smiled, that superior smug smile he loved so much.

The Nun took the slip, spun without any effort, and glided back out the front door, as if floating on air. Jim was clearly unnerved by the maner of her exit, he never actually saw her open the door, but the feel of a wad of money reassured him. As the door silently closed behind her, Jim became aware of a sudden buzz of conspiratorial whispering from his punters as they all, but one, fled the shop.

Yet again Jim was a little disconcerted, and then a crazy thought grabbed his attention. They had all heard the bet, and they actually believed it. They believed the world was going to end, and were all off down the pub to drink themselves silly before the event. Losers.

The End of The World

Jim's ponderings were cut short when realised that his last punter stood at the counter before him. He should have guessed, "Lucky" Leo, the biggest loser in town, the one who could never leave the shop until all his money was gone, was the last one.

"What's this Lucky, the last race is just about to start, are you going to finally win big, now that everybody else have gone off to get drunk before the end of the world – the bloody losers, ah, just cause a silly Nun had a bad dream."

"No Jim, just cash my winnings, and I'm off home, before that Nun comes back for her winnings"

"What, you as well" Now Jim was well and truly discombobulated. Handing money to Leo was something he could never, ever remember doing before.

"What's got into you all" Jim added.

"I want to get my money before 'The End of the World', the odds on favourite runs, in the two horse 5:45 at Doncaster, for which YOU gave odds of a million to one... Bye Jim, see you in hell".

The Pact

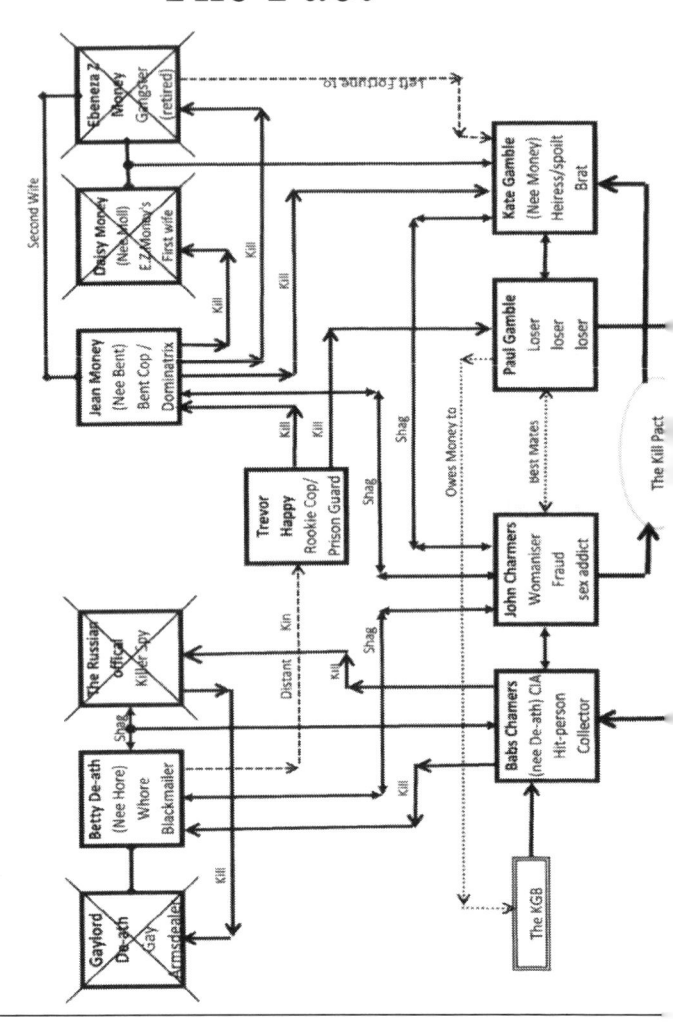

The Pact

<u>Date : Friday 22nd March.</u>
<u>Location: A Bar in town</u>

John Charmer and Paul Gamble sat in a private booth. They were having their usual end of week, after work, binge drinking session. But this session was not quite like usual, a decision was made, and the pact was agreed. The Pact promised to end all their problems...Promised?

<u>Saturday 1st April   In John & Babs Charmers' House</u>

Betty De-Ath sat on a stool in her daughter's Kitchen... And waited.

She was waiting for her daughter to return, to confront her with bad news. It was a stupid mistake, on her part, but she felt that she had to tell her only child to go...run... and quick. The Russians were coming. Betty felt total responsible for what Babs had become, after all, she had introduced her to 'friends' in the CIA. She was wrong to believe her little darling would be a carbon copy of herself.

While she sat there, she mused upon what had brought her to this point.

The Pact

Betty had done a good deal of 'work' for the agency during the McCarthy era, the 'reds under the bed' hysteria. It was not really work in her eyes – seducing Russian diplomats, and American citizens 'suspected' of communist leanings – that she considered fun. She had previously been a high class whore, and was proud of her seduction success rate – not far off 100 percent. The number of suicides that occurred because of her activities did not faze her; she considered that most of them should be classed as 'assisted'.

Her mind drifted back to her two 'failures' in her craft. The first: A minor Russian Cossack Diplomat suspected of spying. He seduced her before she managed to get her weapons out, and she fell in 'love'...sorry – into lust, got sloppy, messy, and very pregnant. The second: Gaylord De-Ath, a dodgy arms dealer, and ...Of course, gay. The latter fact she deduced purely from her failure to charm his pants down no matter how she tried. Due to the fact that he was gay, but terrified of anyone knowing of his orientation, dead rich, and added to that - Betty had realised she was starting to 'show', they got married. They got married to cover up their 'cock-up's', so to speak.

The Pact

She thought it prudent at that point in her career to retire from the communist witch hunt as it, and she, were going out of fashion. After her child was born, she was prone to get bored (You can read that last bit any way you wish), so she would hire herself out to help along divorce cases, and such like.

Things carried on quietly enough until Gaylord sold some dodgy armaments to an even dodgier Russian backed ~~terrorist~~ resistance group which blew up in their faces *(again – you can read that whichever way you like)*. It was an accident he claimed, not knowing that Betty had mixed up his papers out of spite after an argument about her getting 'bored'. It was her Cossack lover who took Russia's revenge upon her unfortunate husband. It was a big funeral, but nobody really cried real tears.

Betty was on the point of defecting into the arms of her lover when the CIA sent an assassin for to inflict revenge on the revenge for the accident they presumed was on purpose. At this point, Betty had not yet realised that her own daughter had become a CIA hit-man, sorry... Person. Even once she discovered her daughters new profession, she still could not bring herself to believe that her own daughter could be the one to kill her own father... not that she had ever been told that the Russian was her father. But the thought

The Pact

festered. Then, this very morning, when Betty was shagging her husband... that's Babs husband, John, in Babs bed, he told her of a case full of trophies from his wife's 'Hits'. John said that he had been threatened with the same fate if he ever looked for sex with Babs again. Betty became determined to find out the truth. After she exhausted John, she excused herself, and went and searched. She found the trophy case with ease, and within it she found a host of dismembered manhood's perfectly preserved, in their full glory. Now she knew why the CIA had dumped Babs, she enjoyed her job too much. She even recognised a few, *'arh'* she thought *'I knew they weren't suicides'*. Then she saw it, her favourite, unmistakeable, it was his, *'my precious'* she mused. She was stunned, then she heard John come bounding down stairs, and she pocketed it *(the precious)*, closed the case and walked out in to the hall in a daze. John threw the rest of her clothes at her, and told her to hurry up, Babs was due back, and he had to be somewhere else. She allowed herself to be chivvied out the door and in to her car. She drove round the block, pulled into an alley way, and screamed every obscenity she knew in every language she knew, and some she did not know. She smashed her fists into every piece of padding in reach. Then she reached for her phone, and tapped in the numbers her Russian lover had given her for

The Pact

'emergencies' and blew her daughters cover. She set off home with a satisfied feeling in her gut that she will get her revenge for the revenge for the revenge for the accident...that she caused. That last bit gave her pause, a tinge of guilt, it was all her own fault. She stopped, and turned the car to return to the Charmers' house via the back way, broke in and was now sitting... waiting.

Monday 10th April   On stake out somewhere

Police Chief Jean Bent stood enjoying the thrill of the moment....waiting. She had a rookie cop for company, his name was not relevant in her mind, but we shall call him Trevor Happy, 'Trigger' to his colleagues. He was not a happy boy in that moment, because Jean had him where she wanted, on his knees with his tongue tickling her fancy, as she called it. It's not that he was satisfying her sexually – she wanted far more than his feeble efforts, but she knew he hated it. She had total power over the scared wimp, and he would react just as she wanted him to when the time came.

Her mind drifted to think of another rookie, just like this one, that had purformed all as she asked a few years ago. That obedient dolt killed the wife of the most powerful gangster in the city (so powerful he had

The Pact

become respectable). Daisy Money, wife of Edward Zac Money (E.Z. to his 'friends'), was shot dead by 'accident' in a bungled attempt to plant evidence by a 'rogue' cop at the Money Mansion. Before the cop could be questioned (according to the report) Jean Bent shot him dead in a 'shoot-out' (in which she fired all the bullets). This rookie before her now she considered even feebler than his predecessor. Her mind moved on to E.Z. Now he was a decent lover, and had employed her talents as a dominatrix for some years before (sometimes even the toughest bad guys want be punished). He was so taken with Jean's 'efficiency', and she reminded him of his mother, who he missed terribly, that the two married pronto – Burying Daisy first though.

This coupling never went down too well with E.Z's only daughter, Kate, a spoiled brat of a girl. Her mother, Daisy, had been a pretty airhead with no motherly instinct, or feeling for, or desire to control the girl, so all was left to fawning lackeys.

The marriage did not last long, due to Kate continually putting doubt into her father's mind regarding Daisy's killing. E.Z made the mistake that Jean had genuine feelings for him, but it was only his money she wanted. The inquest concluded he fell down the stairs after drinking excessively on the anniversary of his beloved

The Pact

Mothers death. By this time, Jean had discovered that the city coroner, the D.A. and a few other officials had the same sexual perversions as her now deceased husband.

E.Z. Money's funeral was a big affair, but nobody really cried real tears.

Kate rage at her father's death was quickly mollified by the news that he had left everything to her – Jean got nothing, except for a couple of files containing evidence against a few Judges regarding under-aged sex slaves. She decided to hold on to the files in case she ever got found out. Kate meanwhile, politely, accompanied by veiled threats and laughter, threw her out of the mansion.

Jean vowed she'd find a way to make Kate pay, and introducing her to Paul Gamble was the first step – one she regretted bitterly now. But then again Paul she found John Charmers, his best mate, who just loved her as a dominatrix, and he was so much than this clod. She thought about John down where the rookie was now, and came in the surprised boys face. Her glee at his gagging was disturbed by a noise outside. "Wipe your face, boy, and be quiet" She 'adjusted' her clothing, and waited.

The Pact

<u>Still Mon 10th April In John Charmers & Paul Gamble's Shared Office</u>

John Charmers sat at his desk... Waiting. He was waiting for his long term pal, and work colleague, Paul Gamble. Paul was late, but, then again, he was always late, and today he excelled in his tardiness.

'*Did he know'* thought John?

It was Johns first day back after a week's leave of absence taken for the death of his wife, and he was dreading Pauls arrival. Today would mark the final and irrevocable ending of that friendship...one way or another. It was a friendship that on reflection should never have worked. Paul was lazy, sloppy, and lacked any sort of work ethic. He was, in all aspects of life, a gambler, by name and nature. He was trouble, and John was always the one to fix things. John liked sure things – certainties. Not that life ran that way for him.

'Take my wife... please'(the old jokes were the best, according to John). Babs was loaded, in the bank, and up front (another old joke), just the way he liked his women. Unfortunately, Babs kept her assets tightly rationed at virtual starvation levels, which was exactly the reverse of what he liked in his 'bitches'. He blamed Paul for him getting hitched into a loveless marriage.

The Pact

For John, LOVE = Money + SEX, in any order, and in large quantities, feelings did not come in to it.

The only advantage to having Paul around in work, was he would be the one to cover his absences. It meant that there was no need to worry that his accounting 'methods' would be found out. So, the money side of his life was made bearable...for now, but not for ever.

And Sex.... Well, John lived up to his name too, he was a charmer. Paul had said of him he could charm the knickers of the statue of a sainted nun. John reflected that making Paul his best man was probably the worst thing he ever did. That was until he discovered Babs profession, after a conjugal rites row.

John had a thing for friends wives, and any woman who could claim the title Mother-in-Law, including his own. Betty (Babs mother) didn't like to think that her daughter was not giving her husband everything that he wanted. She, being a semi-retired high class whore, who prided herself on her customer service. She still made him pay (though he did get family rate – A bottle of Hendricks Gin usually did the trick, for the tricks). He had no doubt she would still have wanted to give 'service' even if Babs had not preferred dismembering cocks rather than giving them a good ole suck.

The Pact

Then there was Kate, the heiress, airhead, blonde sex bomb (passive) – no one could lie there and take it so attractively. How the hell did Paul grab her as a prize, and then get him to be best man at the wedding. Still, John thought, he proved the accuracy of that title on the night, while Paul tried to gamble his wife's entire fortune away... and lost...meaning he won, and then went on a two day bender, leaving John to 'Stand' in for him. By the end of the second day John did get a little bored with her just laying there groaning 'more, more', the lazy bitch.

But then there was her mother, Kates' step mother to be precise. She was the total opposite to her daughter, she was the dominant type, and took care of Johns S&M fantasies. Jean Bent was a cop and well used to handing out punishments, whether deserved or not. She rarely let the law, or justice stand in her way of what she desired. Between these three women, John got all the sexual gratification he could need. What more could a man want?

MONEY – that's what, but if today goes to plan he could be well on the way to solving his financial desires. He will be set for life, and he can always get other women.

Meanwhile, he sat...And waited.

The Pact

His revelry was broken by the noise of the office door opening, and Paul slouching in.

"Morning John" said Paul.

"Morning Paul" responded John, a little moodily.

"How was your weekend John" Paul was adding his own undertone too.

"Usual, Quiet" said John, knowing that's not what Paul wanted to hear. "Yours?"

"Grand… and quiet" Paul wasn't going to break first he decided. "The Wife?"

'Ah' thought John, *Now it starts* "Still dead, Paul" he said "and thanks, by the way" His expression of thanks didn't sound very convincing "Yours?" he added, knowing he didn't want to hear the answer.

"Oh, the same" he reposted, with a hint of disappointment. "As always, that is, John" and that was an accusation.

"Ah, sorry to hear that" said John, with a touch of embarrassment. "It didn't work then, Paul, sorry" John didn't mean that at all.

"Oh yes it did, John, your plan lit up the night sky for miles around, though how you knew Kate's gangster

The Pact

father had hid a great pile of explosives in the cabin, I just can't guess...Shame Kate wasn't there, John" Paul had a strange expression which didn't quite match the disappointment he thought should would be showing.

"Oh" John offered, more to fill the gap. Paul seemed to be expecting something.

"Aren't you going to ask why she wasn't there John?" Paul didn't give John a chance to answer. "Seems your charms aren't quite what they used to be John. Kate came home early...in a rage, I thought she rumbled you, now we're in trouble, I thought. When I asked her what was wrong, she just cursed her stepmother and lap-dog, for stopping her 'fun'. At first I thought that she found you there shagging her mum, wouldn't put it past you, you ole dog, but no seems it was that rookie cop she drags around everywhere...poor sod." He paused for effect, but got none. "She then glares at me and the lads as if it was our fault, frightened the lads, they made their lame excuses and bailed. I was on a winning streak John, a winning streak, it's not fair..." Paul had lost the track of his monologue.

"Em" John started, not sure what was coming

"Anyway, then, this morning she gets an irate phone call, could hear the guy shouting down the phone, from

The Pact

the owner of a neighbouring cabin on the lake, complaining his cabin lost all it's windows and half the roof when her cabin blew up last night, and what was she going to do about it, she didn't say a word" Paul breathed "but I could see her expression slowly, very slowly, change from shock to pure delight, and she cut the guy off while he was still ranting. And she did a little dance, she 'danced' across the floor singing a little song, John...and do you know what she was singing John" John tried to respond in the negative but Paul just carried on "Ding Dong the Witch is dead John, she had a grin a mile wide John" Paul stopped momentarily but when John just looked back with furrowed brow, he set off again "You got the mama witch, the evil one, the devil woman herself" John remained in neutral, to Pauls annoyance "You have killed Jean Bent in that cabin, John, bit of a bonus really. I mean if you had of managed to actually kill Kate, that bitch would have tried to move heaven and earth to stitch me up for it, while digging to find the true culprit and congratulate him with a bullet through the head to keep him quiet. Now the coast is clear...."

John kept quiet; he judged Paul still had more to say.

"Though... I wouldn't wait too long. Kate may be an airhead, but if the cops start asking too many questions, your involvement might start troubling her –

The Pact

it was your idea to get her there I presume. She might try and put 2 and 2 together and get 3.9, you never know. So don't wait, but let me get my alibi in order."

John was posed to speak when Paul added in a half dream "Still a shame about your plan – it was a corker – but you're a clever lad I'm sure you'll think of something... But quick you know".

"Ah, Paul, about that, you know" John hesitated, Paul is not going to like this "I don't think I can do it, Paul, sorry" John was avoiding eye contact with him; they had been best mates for so long, but not anymore. Paul was speechless. "I know I've let you down, but I just can't do it, I've lost the nerve."

John had hit the trigger, Paul looked like he was going to explode.

"John, we had an agreement, I kill your wife, and you kill mine. I've lived up to my end of the bargain, now it's overdue that you do your bit. The Mother-in-law doesn't count, but with her out the way it should be a lot easier, no hard-arsed bitch of a Police Chief looking for her daughter's killer. Don't get me wrong, I'm extremely grateful for her demise, but it doesn't change the fact that I've killed your wife, now you must do for mine." Paul rested his case.

The Pact

"I never actually agreed to this deal, Paul, I never thought you were serious. I thought it was just the drink talking" John did not like the look on Pauls face.

He leaned forward into Johns face. "I was, and am deadly serious, make no mistake, John"

At that very moment, a door from the next office burst open, and in strode a fierce looking woman, accompanied by a young and very nervous uniform cop.

"Paul Gamble, I'm arresting you for the murder of Barbara Chambers, anything you…" Paul didn't hear the rest of the standard spiel, he was stunned. Firstly, by the appearance of the Mother-in-law he had presumed he was free of, Police Chief Jean Bent, alive and well. Next, it dawned on him that he'd been set up, John had betrayed him big time, his best mate. His astonishment changed to fear of consequences, then to white hot anger. "You bastard!" He exploded out of his seat to try and throttle John, as he did so his quick mind realised his mistake. The now terrified rookie cop, pulled his gun and fired, just as he was supposed to.

As Paul fell to the floor, he realised just how much he'd been used, but he knew he'd have the last laugh. In the brief moment of his remaining life, his recent history flashed before his eyes. It was not a pleasant sight, just a list of screw-ups.
Gambling was his ruin; he had stupidly lost every

The Pact

penny of his wife's fortune, and more, to the wrong people: people with Russian accents, and nasty temperaments. This is so wrong he thought. The pact with John should have been so simple. He kills Babs in a staged robbery gone wrong, and Russians forgive his debt, then John kills Kate, and Paul collects the insurance, and all his problems are solved. Should have guessed John was Jeans lap dog, and shagging Kate as well. Why did he ever think John would go through with it? He cursed his own impatience, should have waited for John to act instead of thinking that if he did for Babs it would force Johns hand. His pathetic attempt to kill Babs came to his mind. A bloody CIA agent... Babs... that explained the Russians demands, and the ease with which she had disarmed him... Well, he was distracted by the sight of Betty's body sprawled on the kitchen floor. He remembered thinking that nobody should have their head at that angle to her body. Babs explained to him that she had had an argument over Sexual obligations/orientations/KGB Agents/dismembered manhood's or some such, and the amount of gin Betty drunk. She said that the Russkies were on to her, so it was time for her to disappear. She also explained to Paul how he was to set up the place for a gas explosion, so that Betty's body could be mistaken for hers, and that he was to carry on as if he'd been totally successful in his side of the pact. She also explained, down the barrel of a gun, that if he failed in that task, or blabbed about this new pact, that she would return to wreak an extremely horrible revenge upon him, which she helped to reinforce by showing off her collection of trophies

The Pact

(which was the only thing she was taking with her).
With his last breath he almost managed a chuckle. To know that John would have a bad experience at the bank, and Paul wouldn't be around to stop that note going to their company's CEO (insurance against John ratting on him). The thought that Kate would be broke, and her step mother wouldn't get a bean, and for Babs, the Russians never believe he'd done the job. He died smiling strangely.

Meanwhile, Trevor Happy, had turned on his heels, and burst out of the room. John and Jean heard him puking his guts up in the next room, although whether it was the killing or his earlier efforts that made him sick, Trevor never admitted.

Jean put her fingers to her lips to hush John, kicked Paul's grinning face to make sure he wasn't faking death. She motioned for John to leave the room, which he did as if in a dream. When they passed an empty room, Jean grabbed Johns arm and pulled him in, shutting the door behind them. "Well, that worked well" said Jean "Now prove to me you're worth my efforts, John"

"I will if you will" John replied sinking to his knees.

When they finally had nothing left to prove, they 'adjusted' their clothing.

The Pact

"My brat of a step daughter had better not hear about this, do you still intend to marry Kate".

"Of course, Jean, it was part of our pact; Paul knocks off my wife, then we set him up for the blame, you arranged his termination. Now; me and Kate are free to marry, I take control of the estate, Kate has a tragic accident, and I seek solace in your bed. Sorted. But why did you blow up the cabin, Jean?" She smiled that disturbing smile of hers and left the room to 'do her job'.

She was thinking as she walked away. '*If John thinks he's going to last long in our marriage, he's got another thing coming... another even more tragic accident, and the whole lots mine. Sorted proper'*.

Sunday 16th Apr   Outside the Money Mansion

Jean had been getting calls from John and from Kate. John she didn't bother with, he would only be looking for a good whipping, so to speak, but for Kate to call was rare. Jean knew Kate had gone into a mighty sulk when she found out that news of her own death was proved to her to be premature, so what on earth is she wanting to talk about, can't be good whatever it is, '*better go round and shut her up'*. Jean was shocked to

The Pact

find Kate's house stripped bare, and Kate screaming and shouting at her to get everything back, pronto, or else she would blab about how Jean killed her father. To find out that her dead husband's fortune had disappeared thanks to her brainless daughter's stupidity in marrying in Paul Gamble, was bad enough, but to have Kate threaten her was too much. The fact that she had got the two together in the first place she conveniently forgot. The amount of effort she had put in to catching that disgusting man and then disposing of him she considered was the pinnacle of her achievements (along with not getting caught for being bent) and this one had Fucked it all up. So she did what she had always wanted to do, and blew the girl's brains out. Of course she had never intended to do the deed in front of witnesses, "*Oh well – Now I've really fucked it*" she thought. Jean cursed the fact she had stopped John going to complete his side of the pact with Paul, she'd put the idea of greater gains to be had by John. '*Still he was too gutless to go through with it anyway'.* Her next thought was about prison and of all the people she'd banged up there. She was going to be '*Fucked, good and proper'.* So when a young nervous cop shouted from behind her to drop her gun, she got really narked, "Fuck you, kid" and turned in a rage of anger.

The Pact

Trevor Happy lived up to his nick name, then puked his guts up again, twice in a matter of days '*God, will I ever get used to this?*' Shortly afterwards he quit the police force to become a prison guard.

Jean's funeral was a small affair; no one turned up, so only the funeral director cried, when he realised there was nobody to pay his bill.

<u>Monday 17th April   At   an   International   Airport Terminal departure lounge</u>

John stood in the terminal...waiting. For what, he did not know. '*Where did it all go wrong?*' He had had no intention of going through with a marriage to Kate, not while Jean was around. That one was always up to no good, and her smile terrified him. It was always his intention to grab Babs money and run. It was only a matter of time before his company fraud was found out. Now he was trying to run. But all the money was gone.

He had not learned that his wife's accounts had been cleared until after Paul's death. Had Paul betrayed him, but how? Kate kept ringing, and ringing him, sobbing and screaming down the phone. It wasn't the loss of her husband she was bemoaning, Oh no. It was the fact that the bailiffs were at her door to take everything, and throw her out of the house, and John

The Pact

had to come round and fix it. He fixed it by dumping his phone, since Jean and Betty were not answering; he felt it pointless keeping it. He'd only just avoided the police – seems they raided his office, and found evidence of fraud. Paul again – he knew all the while – the bastard.

The police found him crying in the toilets, he'd shat himself when he was spotted. According to one officer he had been repeating "Please let there be women" over and over again.

Friday 21st April   somewhere in the South Pacific

Babs Chambers (Now calling herself Betty De-Ath) sat at a beach bar studying the internet. She was looking for any news of home. She had seen news of Paul's demise. When she saw that Jean Bent been killed by a cop after killing her own step-daughter she burst into laughter. With her husband on his way to prison it was time to celebrate. She looked around the bar, and a slim and very pretty young girl caught her eye. She was alone and looked bored; Babs, sorry Betty, decided *'she's mine'* and moved in for the kill. Little did she know that the girl was part of joint CIA/KGB team sent to , finally enact the revenge for the revenge...etc.

The Pact

Nothing was known of Babs fate at the time, but rest assured it wasn't pleasant....

One Year Later   In a 'Correctional Facility'

By strange coincidence, a distant nephew of Betty De-Ath worked as a guard in the same prison in which John Charmers was incarcerated. It was he who was on duty in the visitor's room when John got a visit from Betty De-Ath's lawyer. The lawyer had told him that a badly mutilated body had been discovered on a tropical pacific island. The body's DNA was close enough to Betty's to be hers, and since she had been missing for a year she had been declared dead. He then told him that John, as closest living relative, would inherit her entire fortune. John was seen to break down sobbing, and distraught, according to a witness, that same guard. John had been accused of killing of a fellow inmate in the shower (he claimed it was an accident) so was facing another trial. It was said that the news had been too much for him after he was found hanging in his cell, coincidently by that same nephew, who... would you believe it... became the next in line for the fortune. The name of that guard was Trevor Happy, 'Go lucky' to his colleagues.

Trevor Happy decided, after 'witnessing' the tragic death, that being a guard was not for him and he left to

The Pact

be...to be a long way away before any questions were asked.

It's a funny old world

Desire

You are on my mind.
Can't shake you off, or pass you by.
Don't get me wrong,
I want what you can give me.
But can I take the pain,
Of what you want in return.
Every time you satisfy my desires,
You strip something from me.
Now, I stand before you,
And you can see what I want.
I probe your sensitive parts,
In hope of your acquiescence.
Will your lips accept my advances?
My fingers caressing, teasing, your buttons.
Will I unlock your heart?
Can I make you come gushing forth with your bounty
Or have I overspent my welcome,
You, sending me home, tail between my legs.
I wait in fevered anticipation,
And then the crushing blow.
You say I
"have insufficient funds for this transaction"
You spit out my card
Oh well – off home I go for another night Watching
"Strictly" with the wife

"Nasty Weather We're Having"

"Nasty Weather We're Having"

Tom lived in the big city. Perhaps I should say – existed, for his life had a simplicity to it: Sleep, wake, shit, wash (optional), eat, dress(if required), walk, work, piss, drink, work, walk, drink, walk, drink, eat (optional), drink, undress(maybe), pass out, repeat. Life was a blur. Despite all this: Somehow he managed to keep his job. Sometimes he remembered what his job was. Sometimes he remembered where he lived, that is to say he often wake up in familiar surroundings even if he had no recollection of how that came to pass. Why did he drink so much? Well if it was to forget, it appears that part actually worked.

Some woman...his Mother? Sister? Wife?...had always been at him to stop, sort himself out before he got locked away. But the simple, sodden, solitary existence was one he claimed he preferred, as long as the CIA let him spout his conspiracy theories, like the president of the US was hardly even human, with only half a brain, and an inability to speak the truth. At times he himself was surprised he had not been whisked off to a secret location to be tortured. Although, with his blackouts after his drinking sessions...may be had had?

What of his home life: Well, his apartment was in a rundown part of the suburbs. It was in the basement of an old, somewhat dilapidated, detached building. A building, according to him, that was populated by a

"Nasty Weather We're Having"

bunch of very strange characters. All aliens the lot of them, especially the landlord... lizard like, insectoids, arachnids, Albanians, or some such. All part of the invasion, he had heard some Republican politician going on about. He was convinced they were on to him, believed that when the landlord started installing smoke detectors, fire alarms, and extinguishers all over the building that they were actually installing spy cams, and listening devices. Later it occurred to him that, maybe, just maybe, that they were afraid of fire. Now he knew their weakness, fire, and for the first time he felt that he had the edge on them. So he went out to get drunk as a celebration, or was it to forget... He could not remember anyway.

So, a simple, sodden, solitary existence...

Then the alien space ship arrived. Again!

Nobody had believed him the first time, when he rolled in to work after a five day bender looking like he'd been pulled through a space ship backwards. The Alien Abduction excuse for being late to work after a good night out, had never worked for anybody before, but somehow he got away with it, that is to say, he didn't get fired then and there. Well, it was a government job.

"Nasty Weather We're Having"

The second time was a very different affair. He was relatively sober when the event occurred, as he had just finished 'work' for the day. Normally that would not be the case (Sobriety that is) since he usually was equipped with at least one hip flask full of strong spirits to help him through the afternoon. This day he had forgotten his flask. (*Note: It should be clarified – forgotten – it's not the case that he would ever consciously remember to fill and place about his person that container of lubricant for the afternoon. This was purely muscle memory. This day his Alien implant was playing up so he thought, and the full flask was left on the counter*).

So he left his place of work un-anesthetized, and semi-aware of his surroundings, and hating it. On walking to his first watering hole on his zigzag route home, he became aware of a darkening of the street. Looking up he saw a huge space ship moving across the sky above the city, blocking out the light. It brought a whole ominous and thunderous weather system with it. Big black rolling clouds engulfed it, more or less hiding it from view. He remembered standing on the street, staring up at the sky. Wild lightening stabbed down at the skyscrapers. People were rushing passed, heads bent, ignoring the sight. He pointed unsteadily at the light show, and attempted to attract attention to the invasion, but his semi-sober brain was not used to

"Nasty Weather We're Having"

words enough to be understood. Most of his audience wrote him off as another drunken nutter and walked passed at a faster pace.

"Nasty weather we're having, you better get off home before you get struck" was a half concerned passerby's comment. 'They don't see it' Tom managed to think.

He woke the following morning in an alleyway. The storm still rumbled overhead, without any light show, just dark clouds, and nothing else to see. He rose stiffly, and staggered, still drunk from his previous night efforts to inform every patron of every bar in the city of the coming invasion and how to defeat then Being now daylight, despite the efforts of the storm clouds, he made his way back in the direction of his work place.

At the sight, and sound of him as he tried to alert everyone in the office to the invasion, he was dragged into his bosses' office. Big Boss Bertha called his Alien invasion story even weaker than his abduction tale. But he did not give in, and showed her the place the aliens had put the implant. The sight of his spotty full mooning arse was the final straw for her, she had him escorted from the building, telling him never to darken its door again.

"Nasty Weather We're Having"

He slumped on a park bench across the road from the office, feeling worse for wear. His brain was struggling to cope with his new situation. He thought of hitting the bars again, but what with. He was broke, friendless, hung-over, jobless, and if he didn't come up with the rent he owed by the end of day, he'd be homeless too – he remembered that much. Tom had accused his 'bastard' landlord, of being more lizard than human, and being part of the invasion, though invasion of what he wasn't too sure, foreigners, aliens, killer bees...lizards?, he felt he had forgotten something important.

Got to stop drinking, was the thought of the day, possibly again, he couldn't remember. Got to sort myself out, made himself think of starting drinking again.

Sleep...Yes sleep first...sleep would be good. For the first time that he could remember, he trudged the trudge home without stopping at a watering hole on the way, in daylight. Of course, he didn't remember much before this day anyway.

At the end of his street he stopped. Fire engines and police cars thronged the road around the ruined building which had contained his apartment. He rushed forward.

"Nasty Weather We're Having"

"You can't go in there sir" a cop shouted.

"I live there" he, sort of, lied, as he stumbled across a barrier in his way.

The cop grabbed him with ease before gasping at the smell of him. "Which apartment" he asked.

"Basement" Tom mumbled.

"That's where the fire started, sir, place doused in petrol, and set alight."

"Its those bastard aliens, they own the building" he alleged, not sure why, "for the insurance" he added.

"Why is it you stink of petrol your self... sir" He renewed his grip on Tom "I think you need to come to the station with us, sir, to answer a few questions".

Tom was cuffed and bundled towards a waiting police van.

"It's the invasion, the alien invasion, it's started" The drink took over his addled brain. "They don't like fire" was the last outburst he managed

The officer pushed his head down and unceremoniously bundled him into the back of the van. The doors slammed closed leaving him in the dark, as the van drove off. It made for a quiet part of town

"Nasty Weather We're Having"

before completing a vertical takeoff, and spiralled up to disappear into the cloud still covering the city.

I Tell You No Lie!

I Tell You No Lie

"It was the fairies at the bottom of the garden...they did for The Mother!"
That was what I shouted, nervously, at the two Gardaí as they burst onto the scene. I stood there frozen, standing as I was, over the recumbent mound that, just moments previously, had been the menacing form of The Mother, towering over me.
I knew by the looks on their faces that I was going to have a hard time convincing them with that line of defence.
It was a lie, of course, and a bad one. Fairies would not have the strength or concentration to have lifted the gun and fired, but I couldn't have told them about the goblin, 'cause that nasty boy would never have forgiven me. He would have my guts for garters. Quite literally!

The Mothers limp form was declared still breathing, as, miraculously, an ambulance appeared, disgorging paramedics. It took a great deal of heaving, moaning, complaining, and cries for assistance to get her massiveness into the back of the ambulance, which then gingerly set off down the lane.
In the meantime I was pushed down into the back seat of the Garda car, carefully to make sure that my head made heavy contact with the door post. My moans of protest and pain were drowned out by one Garda proudly telling me how lucky I was, because we were going to the brand spanking new Garda Station, far more spacious and comfortable than the old damp hole they used to have. On arrival, I was given the grand tour of the more private areas where only "The

I Tell You No Lie

long arm of the Law" and those "Known" to it would normally have seen. I was invited to take a seat in a small room. And then they began.

"You're in big trouble, *boy!*" spat the bad cop, "we got you banged to rights." Whatever that meant.
Good cop tried a different approach. "Come on lad, just tell the truth, I'm sure you didn't mean it. It was an accident, right?" She put on her best disarming smile, meant to melt my heart. Little did she know!
I stuck to my guns…but not the one the goblin used to put several well placed holes in The Mothers head.

I called her "The Mother" but as I was a goblin changeling it's not an entirely correct title, blood wise. The old crone never gave birth to me. How do I know this, you ask? Did the goblins tell me themselves? Oh no, it came from her lips every time I transgressed her punitive rules. "You're no son of mine," she would exclaim, and alternatively, "I curse the day you were laid at my door."
Since I could find no birth cert (in a search of her files while she slept) I must be a changeling. I will brook no other explanation – so there!

"This gun's got your prints all over it, I bet." Bad Cop was at it again. It seemed more of a threat than an actual belief, as he waved the bagged weapon that had been lying at my feet. "And with your form… open and shut case, I'm thinking." Sod the bastard for reminding me of that!

I Tell You No Lie

That gun was Grandpa's old vampire hunting revolver with the silver bullets. Oh, the tales he used to spin about his young days hunting down those "foreign blood sucking devils" which I presumed must be vampires. He used to show me and let me play with it when I was very young. Stupid idiot, should never have left it loaded. I miss Grandpa a great deal, wish I had done that time as well.

"Look, you can change your story, you were probably in shock when you realised what had happened, and we won't mention the fairies in our report." Good Cop this time. Still, there's no way I'm ratting on the goblin, and it's true I was in shock - didn't think anything could poleaxe her like that. Too late to change the culprits to pixies – might have got away with the pixies first time!

But why goblins – what had they got against The "Mother"?

Well, it all stems from the time that Dad disappeared. It was around that time that The Mother got that "fit" young man to redo the patio. You see, Dad was friendly with the goblins – sort of, that is to say they were frequent visitors to his man-shed of an evening. I know that, of course, because he told me so, in a roundabout fashion. You see, Dad was fond of a drink, or two... or more, somewhat partial to the Guinness, keeping a plentiful supply of the canned draught stuff in a beer fridge in the shed. So when the thirst would take him, outside of pub hours, (usually the moment the Mother opened her cavernous mouth) he'd take

I Tell You No Lie

himself off to his sanctuary at the bottom of the garden, to evade her scorn.
She did not like, or approve of his drinking, her being teetotal, and from a piously religious family littered with kiddie fiddling priests and whipping nuns. She would often remonstrate with him over the dreaded drink.
I asked him one day why he drunk so much – His reply was, "It's not all me – it's the goblins"
"The goblins?" I would return incredulously – as you would.
"The goblins" he would assure me. "Have to keep 'em sweet, or they'd wreck the lawn."
"Don't you mean moles?" I would speculate, re. lawn damage.
"No! They don't drink CANNED Guinness!" was his strident reply, while looking at me as if I was a total idiot. There ended the discussion. What moles actually drink was never revealed to me.
I used to sneak into his shed while he was still in the pub, to see if I could catch a goblin, and interrogate it about my heritage, but never found one. Then Dad caught me in there – I'll say nothing further about that.

"We know it must have been tough what with your father being a drunken bastard" It was Good Cop again "and him vanishing LIKE THAT… You can tell us, it'll be alright." What? Did she guess something about the patio?

At this point, I suppose I should fill you in about this family that I was dredged up in.

I Tell You No Lie

The Mother was the outcome of an illicit romance between her banshee mother ("that woman" as Dad would refer to her) and a small hillock (possibly related to Forth Mountain) according to Dad. She had a voice that could cut stone, and once tried out for a part in a Wexford Opera production of Wagner's 'The Ring'. At first she was enthusiastically welcomed into the cast, until sense prevailed (The cost of reinforcing the stage, replacing all the glass/glasses in the Opera House was too prohibitive. And the damage to the audience…)

Dad, on the other hand, was a happy go unlucky, diminutive bloke (small enough to be covered by just one patio slab). His father – not the gun toting Grandpa mentioned earlier – was a pure born leprechaun. What? You don't believe me? Just look at the cast list for 'Darby O'Gill and the Little People'. There weren't any special digital effects in those days, so the Disney crowd came over to Ireland with promises of pots of gold, and tempted him, and his ilk, away with their lies, never to be seen again outside a film studio. (If you take a look at the credits you'll see there's no actors listed playing leprechauns … See? Told you!).

After the "disappearance" of the little fellow, Mother determined to demolish the shed – "It stinks like a rotten brewery," she claimed "It's got to go"
But what if Dad comes back I pleaded?
"He is not coming back." She nearly knocked me over with the vehemence of her pronouncement. "Is he?" Did I detect her make the slightest of glances in the

I Tell You No Lie

direction of the patio? Unfortunately there's no action replays in real life, so you'll have to take my word on it. In desperation, I blurted out about the goblins, and having to keep a supply of black stuff in the fridge. To save the lawn. I volunteered to keep an eye on them so they didn't get too rowdy … a big mistake!
Her eyes narrowed and slowly she spoke "You needn't be taking on his ways, you're no son of his, so no need to take his place at the bar, boy." The contempt in her snarl confirmed it – I was a changeling!

It was then that the angry goblin appeared, bringing with him the gun I'd hid after Grandpa's unfortunate demise, and before I knew it – bang, bang, bang, and down she went, taking the shed down with her. The ground shook with the impact. Was that what brought the Gardaí so quickly – looking for the source of the earthquake? No. it was The Mother herself and her continual complaints to the police about the foreigners across the road still breathing within a mile of her. Don't get me wrong – she wasn't racially prejudiced, she hated everything that breathed, she hated life itself. It must have been her banshee bloodlessness. Which doesn't explain why I was so splattered with her blood when the cops burst in? Was the banshee bit a lie – was it another lie my Dad told?

"Now look here, me lad'o, you keep these tall tales up, you're gon'a be put away permanently, by the guys in white coats, and there's no coming back from there." That Bad Cop was getting on my nerves. But not as much as good cop was.

I Tell You No Lie

"He's right you know. Keep claiming it was the fairies, and it'll be a straitjacket and padded cell." Fuck her!

I had to do something. Oh, why did I not blame the eastern Europeans across the road? These Gardai are townies, they'd probably have swallowed that, after all The Mother had done to upset them.
It would be too much to hope that the goblins would come to my rescue. I'm going to be punished for their crime.

"We've just had word; your Mother was Dead on arrival at the hospital. Its murder now and you're going to the loony bin for good." I don't suppose it would be the normal way, even for Bad Cop, to tell a son of his mother's death. Good Cop didn't even offer any sympathy – well she did mumble something, but I wasn't listening.

The wicked Witch was dead. Oh sweet joy!

I almost did a little dance. I almost showed my pleasure in a pleased expression – I think you would call it a smile – but I lack the facial muscles to pull it off (my heritage you see). In fact the pain of trying to smile caused me such hurt, I started crying.
Stupid Good Cop patted me on the back saying. "There, there," but Bad Cop was unmoved, he had had enough "Book him, and lock him away."
"With pleasure," said ex-Good Cop, and my fate was sealed.

I Tell You No Lie

Anyway, I'm a changeling, goblin spawn, which means I'm a goblin myself!
And it was a goblin that killed The Mother.

I tell you no lie!

The Torturers Lair

I crept in to the torturers lair
Met by a demon with a deranged stare
Cold sweat dampening my underwear
I whispered out a pitiful prayer
And sank down, down, in a deep despair
Into the forbidding dentists chair

A blinding light in my eye doth shine
As my body starts on its recline
Mouth gaping wide – beyond its design
Tingle running all along my spine
My tormentors face pressed up to mine
The wicked drill– how I sense its whine

T'was ages since the onset of pain
Seared a path betwixt my teeth and brain
Prayed to the dentist with hope in vain
For a quick extraction to keep me sane
But dis-appointment on me did reign
Cos six weeks wait was the ole refrain

Alarm - got call – come in quick
Client cried off feeling sick
Headed off at frantic lick
Driving like a lunatic
Felt I'd fallen for an evil trick
When told I'd just feel a little prick

I wish I'd listened to my ole mum
While laying here with face going numb
Don't eat sweets, or a single cake crumb
Or to this torture you will succumb
for masked raider to extract a sum
From your purse and poorer you'll become

Now my mouth is filled with vast array
Of tools, and fingers, and water spray
Asked "are I going on Holiday"
Before tut, tutting at my x-ray
Then drilling begins, I start to pray
Oh, please, please, please will it go away

As in a pool of cold sweat I lay
"Wider" I'm told, I'm forced to obey
Thou how I did I truly can't say
Thinks – forever open my mouth will stay
Until told "that enough for today"
Tortures over, my mind shouts hooray

But on rising to the upright way
As I spat out my tongue to a tray
The great extractor, to my dismay
Said my teeth are riddled with decay
And have to come back another day
As you go out – don't forget to pay

Time on His Hands

Time on His Hands

"I tell you it's true" said John.
"Don't give me that John, I asked you a simple question, and you come up with nonsense" Kate was having none of it.
"Look Kate, I know it's hard to believe. Sounds ridiculous, but how else could I have learnt Chinese in 5 minutes" John was getting desperate.
"For all I know, you could have been lying about not knowing it in the first place." She was looking at him with a new raised level of suspicion. His drinking and drug 'experiments' had not impressed her lately.
"Oh, come on, I'm a science student, never been into languages, and you've known me since junior school, just stay here for an hour, just an hour, and then you will know" he pleaded.
The pair stood silent for a moment, Kate looked around at the room. It was no more than a bunker, a grubby, stark, and dark cell. John's camping gear; single camp bed, smelly generator, battery lights, single burner stove, fold up table, and one chair. She was truly disappointed, because this was not the experience she had been dreaming of.
"No John, I'm going now" Kate could not have been more emphatic, as she turned and left the room, pushing the door shut, and returned into daylight, tears streaming down her face. John didn't see those tears, he only felt the rejection. He slumped to the floor in a corner, just as he did that night a fortnight ago, the night he discovered the room.
That night he'd been drinking heavily, and taking some dubious tabs procured from an even shadier source. The university were about to chuck him out, if he didn't

Time on His Hands

complete some of his overdue project work, and attend lectures on Monday, and this was Saturday midnight, and he had nothing done. More importantly, to him, the girl of his dreams, the afore mentioned Kate, had been entirely ignoring him. She had been the 'girl next door' in his childhood, always been friends, but he'd wanted more. They had been together at school, and now studying for degrees, despite different subjects, he'd made sure he would be at the same university. Both had been brilliant students – John had a brain the size of a small planet, but Kate was its star. Kate was flying high, not even giving him a nod, and he was struggling – believing he was losing her for good – his work suffered, took to binge drinking and drugs, beginning a spiral downwards.

Then that night, as he explored the ruin of a long-abandoned government research station, looking for a place to hide from the world, he found the dark underground room. He went in, closed the massive door, and using the remaining power on his mobile phone to illuminate the emptiness, found a clean, clear corner and slumped down. Swigging from a spirit bottle, knocking back a handful of the tabs, he sat in the dark, and waited for the world, and his miserable life, to move on and leave him behind. And he sat, while his grandfather's old analogue Rolex, with luminous dial and hands counting away the moments with a smooth sweeping action. And he sat, and drained the last of the cheap whiskey, waiting for the drugs to numb his hurt, and separate him from the world.

Time on His Hands

The next time he touched base with some form of reality, his timepiece claimed 8 hours had past. He was stiff and thirsty, but still resolved to see though his passive 'ending it all' attempt. So, he sat. Occasionally, he would rise, and stretch aching muscles. Then he slept, woke, cramped, stood, stretched, and sat, while granddads watch hands slid round the dial.
John maybe stubborn at times, like that night, but he had too much common sense to be stupid for too long. So after 12 hours had dragged past, "sod it" he thought. He was parched, starving, and totally bored. He gave up, rising with stiffness, and set off back to the surface. He still had some time to get some work done, possibly, but, a late breakfast was first order of business. To his surprise, he didn't find himself blinded by bursting into full daylight. It was still dark, a moonless dark night. "Damn" he muttered, at first believing that his granddads formerly ultra-reliable Rolex had lost half a day. Had incarcerated himself for the full 24-hour job? In a knee-jerk reaction, he checked his phone, which confirmed a time of 5 minutes past midnight, Sunday. He became very confused, if he'd spent a whole day in the hole, why was his phone not dead, as it was very low on charge when he went in. Then: Sunday, how could it still be Sunday, that would mean no time at all had passed Had he imagined it all, what had those tablets done to him?
Oh well, if it is Sunday AM the all-night café down the road would be open, so he resolved to park his confusion for the while, and go and feed his bodily thirst, leaving the mind to stew for a while. The time

Time on His Hands

and day was confirmed on arrival at the watering hole, it was Sunday morning not long past midnight, and he still had a whole day ahead to get something done. He'd got a second chance to keep his place at uni., a whole day to get some work done.

After he'd fed himself to capacity, he returned to his tiny flat, and laid down on the bed. He set the alarm for 7 hours after an argument with himself over how much time was needed, A, for sleep, B, for work, and nestled down to sleep. It was only when he closed his eyes that he realised that he wasn't the least bit sleepy, or even tired, but he did feel dirty. He got up and went into the bathroom. Once there, he stood contemplating a bath, shower, or just face wash, until his eyes focused on the stubbled phizog in the mirror, and froze. Stubble, a full days' worth, or more covered his countenance. He was absolutely convinced he'd shaved before going out to obliterate some brain cells on Saturday night – only a few hours ago. It was his routine, he always shaved, every day, no matter how good or bad he felt, he shaved.

But the growth on his face told a different story, unless those tablets he'd taken contained some growth compound, like 'Miracle Grow'. He stared at his new appearance, perplexed, but strangely pleased at what he saw, it sort of hid his somewhat receding chin, and he liked it.

He chose the shower, then once clean, dry, and not so smelly, with clean clothes (which he was surprised to find he had some) he turned his attention to work. Or at least tried, but the experience of his 'adventure' was disrupting his concentration. It bugged him, what the

Time on His Hands

hell happened in that room, did the place even exist? Was it all hallucination, did he change the watch, he had to find out. He was sure no time had passed in the room, but the watch and the beard confounded him, bugged him, and he had to find out.

So, he decided, there was nothing for it, he had to satisfy his curiosity, and conduct an experiment. Once his phone was fully charged, and a supply of drink and food collected, and packed into a back pack with laptop, batteries, torches, and all things required for work in the hole, picked up a folding chair and table, and set off. He set off to rid his thought of time machines whilst he completed the minimum amount of work to keep him at university, killing two birds with one stone.

It was first light, about 6 am when he shut the door on the outside world. He'd left his phone outside the bunker door, as it was still in touch with the internet, inside there was no signal. *'Ok' he thought 'no internet, never mind, don't need the distraction...Perfect'.* The room had a small toilet off, but with no water to flush, or wash, he'd even thought of bringing toilet roll and wet wipes.

He settled himself down to work, setting a mechanical alarm clock for 12 hours, in case he got carried away or fell asleep. And he worked, burying himself in his project. It was like seeing it properly for the first time, with no distractions. He hand wrote feverishly, not wasting precious power, until he'd got it all worked out, and only then typed it all up. He knew he'd still have to prettify the project with some downloaded illustrations, so he'd need a few hours back at base to finish off.

Time on His Hands

To his surprise, the alarm went off just as he'd finished, and saved his work, with his laptop about to die, perfect.
He gathered up his gear, took a moment to decide he'd have to do this again, that is, if his work was ok. He could get back on track, his first project done, but much more to catch up on.
He left the room, picked up his phone, slightly surprised it was still there. But that surprise was nothing to the shock of seeing it still had a full charge, which in turn was dwarfed by the astonishment of the time. 5 minutes past 6 o'clock, still Sunday morning. No, no, no, this can't be true. He quickly climbed to ground level, and looked for the sun. The day was lightly clouded, but there was the sun, in the right place for just gone 6 in the morning.
He wondered if he'd imagined the whole thing. He took a look in his pack, found his note pad festooned with his writing, page after page. He rushed back to the flat, plugging in his laptop, searching for saved files, and there it was, saved with the time he entered the room, and shut the door.
There was only one explanation now, for him, he discovered a sort of passive time machine. He wondered what sort of experiments they'd been up to in that place, but he had no idea what. The thought of telling anyone was too much for him, he'd be thought mad, no one would give him a chance to prove it. His drug taking and binge drinking would be the excuse for all and sundry to put him down, he wouldn't be taken seriously. No, had have to make sure it always worked, 24 hours a day, 7 days a week. He would have to

Time on His Hands

generate some evidence that would help convince everybody it was true.

So he resolved to return, retry, and get all his project work for the year done, after all, if he convinced the authorities of the rooms properties, he'd probably never see the insides of it again.

And it worked anytime, any day, in the matter of a few days; he'd completed all his project work, and then moved on to some pet projects, like languages, to impress Kate. He wanted to give it one more try to woo her. No more drink, no more drugs, and no more shaving, and very soon he had a full luxuriant beard, (an area he'd never been prolific in). In that time he kitted out the room to his liking, with a generator, exercise bike, and other home comforts for the long stay.

Finally, after two weeks, and 12 languages learnt, he could bear it no longer. He'd have to tell Kate. She'd started noticing him again, and didn't seem to mind spending time in his presence.

So he spilt the beans in a quiet moment when he found himself alone with her. Well, that is, he told he he'd found a special place, a room where fantastic things would happen, and could be achieved, where time would stand still. He couldn't quite bring himself to state the actual facts as he saw them, but she seemed impressed, excited even, and whole hearted agreed to join him on his next venture down to this place of wonderment.

Time on His Hands

So here she was, in the room. John told her the truth the moment they'd entered the room. A time machine, and was she impressed, well not a bit.
"I thought you'd grown some balls, and brought me here for a little romance, or at least a shag, but no, you've been on the drugs again, and lost your stupid shaver." at that she stomped off in a huff. "Men" she thought to herself.
"Women" thought John.
The room lost its magic in John's eyes; he'd lost his love again. He packed up his gear, abandoning the exercise bike, and returned to his little flat, and his old ways, and shaved. Binged drank throughout the rest of the year and more. He never told anyone about his discovery, the room remained his secret.
Meanwhile Kate decided to be gay, as all men are stupid, at least the only one she could ever love certainly was. Her relationships were never very successful – her partners always claiming she wouldn't commit, possibly because they couldn't grow beards.
John woke from his morass after a couple of years, realising how much time he'd lost to drink and drugs. He remembered the room, and decided to revisit. But on arrival back at its location, he found a large government building covering the site. It looked like it had been there for some time.
"Bugger" he thought.

Good v Evil

Good v Evil

Somewhere, deep inside a teaming city, far from the bright lights and prosperity, there lies a filthy crime ridden underbelly. There, in a dark alleyway, half filled with trash, good and evil are embroiled in a deadly daily fight for supremacy.

BIFF... BAFF... BOFF... SLAP... CRUNCH... BANG... BIFF... BONG! Ooo! That one must have hurt!

"Whew, hold on a minute!"

A Super hero paused in his unarmed fight to the death with his arch-enemy. Super Nice Guy was somewhat puffed too by his efforts, and put his hands on his knees gulping for breath.

"I've got a stitch" said Mr Ultimate Evil, his nemesis.

"Me too!" added Super Nice. "Fancy... break, grab... a drink?" he managed.

"Oh, I could murder a pint" gasped Ultimate.

"I was thinking more of a pot of Darjeeling, actually, but if it's a pint you want, you're buying this time"

"What...When have I ever failed to stand my round" said Ultimate to the ground, while spitting little bits of blood.

"Every time MR Ultimate Evil"

"Can you just call me Ultimate, Nice"

Good v Evil

"It's Super Nice to you"

"You're not being super nice to me at the moment, now are you?"

"Ok, Ok sorry, but I don't fancy going in a pub round here, not dressed like this" Nice looked around "Bit rough this".

"It's all right for you; it took me ages to get the makeup right for this look...And some of its tattooed on now. What with the scars an all, one look at me in these places and its fight time again" Ultimate paused for breath. "You can just pull your pants off from over your brown cords, and get rid of the sleeveless pullover"

"What, why?"

"It's got 'Super Nice Guy' knitted into it...front and back." Ultimate looked at Nice again "And the lipstick, eyebrows...lashes? And the wig..." he paused "No your right, but I do know a place we'd both be OK in" Ultimate continued.

"Oh, No! Not that gay bar again! I'd rather take my chances here, and you could be going to a Halloween party" Nice maintained.

"Your joking, It's June, it'll be fight night, with weapons, and this lot will bugger you as soon as they look at you"

"Thanks for caring... but beat me up you mean, surely" Nice tried to correct Ultimate.

Good v Evil

"No I'll get beat up, you'll be buggered for sure. It's a man's world in there, a really rough one. You've never been in prison have you?"

"Neither have you...yet".

"But I've seen it on the Tele, we'd both be safe in the gay bar".

"And THAT's safer for me, for my virginity".

There followed a very short un-pregnant pause.

"You still a virgin Nice?" asked Ultimate with a glint in his eye.

"Arse-wise, yes".

"You've gone red, you're still a virgin, aren't you, come Nice admit it. You are, aren't you".

"Oh shut up, it's all right for you, the girls only like bad boys, don't want to hang around nice guys like me, and being super nice they just think I'm creepy."

Ultimate nodded, as if in agreement, then quickly added "Look, you just haven't met the right girl yet, must be one girl somewhere weird enough to fancy you...anyway, no one will fancy you in the Unicorn, so you're safe"

"Thanks, story of my life. But what about all those gay men".

"Remember, you'll be with me".

Good v Evil

"Oh god, I'll have to go to the jacks with you too".

"Oh well, that's not the best offer I've ever had, but OK if I must."

"Thanks, Ult, you're a saint".

"Oy, pack that in, can't you stop being Super Nice Guy for a minute".

"Sorry.... just joking".

With that, Mr Ultimate Evil led Super Nice Guy through the citys grubby back alleys to the pure filthy Backways Alley and down the dirt strewn steps to the grimy back door of the Unicorn Club. No one in the Unicorn club goes through the front door, thought Nice, erroneously.

Inside was dimly lit, lighting wise, but brightly lit by its clientele. Nice genuinely doubted that anyone in this dive was actually human, but he considered it NOT nice to be unkind to animals, so he smiled his 'Super nice guy' smile at every body, and they all moved away from him as they approached the bar. They took possession of two conveniently, and rapidly, vacated stools at the bar. The barman looked at Nice uneasily, but was reassured that every thing's cool by Ultimate's evil looking physiognomy. As usual, Nice bought the first round, in which Ultimate managed to add a double whiskey chaser for both of them (Knowing full well that Nice won't touch spirits... Well, not until round three).

Good v Evil

The pair chatted, and argued about their afternoons fight and the techniques used. Then moved on to discussing when they were taking their holidays. Nice was concerned that Ultimate wouldn't honour their agreement of taking their sun/beach breaks at the same time, and to totally different places. The thought of Ultimate having free reign in the city without him to keep an eye on his nemesis troubled Nice. In truth though, he wondered what the hell he would do without Ultimates evil ways to battle against.

Gradually the alcohol softened their conversation, and their brains. They started taking about girls, Ultimate admitted he couldn't exactly advise Nice on the subject, since he let slip he'd never "been" with a girl himself. Nice was aghast at the admission. "Look" said Ultimate "I'm only attracted to good girls, the type that will insist on taking you to their parents before getting to first base, so I got no chance".

"What's first base" asked Nice.

"Oh, it's just an expression".

"I know that, what it is I meant?"

Ultimate looked a bit puzzled, and then blurted "Your round I think".

"Oh, again" While Nice tried to attract the barman with his Super Nice Guy look, Ultimate looked around at the denizens of this dive. He grabbed Nice's arm that was waving ineffectually for the barman's attention, and

Good v Evil

said "Don't look now, but there's a couple of birds eyeing us up, I think we're in there."

"What.. Oh...where? " said Nice spinning round.

"I said don't look now, you idiot"

"Sorry... What an odd pair...Them in the corner? A tattooed tart, and a nun out of habit" Nice commented on turning back.

"Odd... Like us you mean?"

"Point taken, you sure they're girls though...And not gay?".

"Both have got tits, the tarts got nowhere in that outfit to hide bollocks, the nuns got her legs clamped together, and they're sitting with a gap between them. Not touching at all!"

"Oh, what do we do, do we go over?"

"Stop staring, Nice you're looking desperate and the Nun one has turned a shade of crimson" then Ultimate added "We'll find out from the barman what they're drinking, buy them refills, and take them over, Oh don't forget to get us chasers this time, make us more manly, I'm going to the gents... wouldn't want to embarrass myself would I".

Nice thought 'suckered again – on my round, he was waiting for my round, Oh boy when this breaks over'...

Good v Evil

The barman finished serving Nice as Ultimate returned. "You bring ours" said Ultimate as he whisked the girls drinks off the bar leaving Nice to struggle with two foaming pints and the chasers.

By the time Nice reached the table, Ultimate had sat next to the 'Nun' leaving only a space next to the scantily clad she devil for him to sit down in, meaning an actual touching of bare flesh would be involved. He tentatively placed the drinks down without looking at the girls and prepared to sit himself, before remembering his manors "Um, sorry... May we join us, I mean you, sorry drinks, all right?" he stumbled, suddenly frightened by the look in the she devils eyes. That look suggested pure evil lust, and he struggled to control himself, down below that is.

"Oh thank you, you're so kind, please make yourself comfortable" The voice was the sweetest and friendliest, and surprising coming from those luscious ruby red lips of the she devil, with a lovely smile in a face half covered in tattoos of scenes of debauchery.

"Fuck off you cunts, all you want is to get us fucking pissed, rip our fucking clothes off and fuck us silly and then go without a fucking good bye" Nice was stunned by the venom in the butter wouldn't melt in the mouth one, but Ultimate looked like he'd fallen head over heels of the girl. The she devil reached over and placed her tattooed hand on the back of the super hero's hand. The physical contact caused blood to circulate in a largely unused area of his body.

Good v Evil

"It's alright, she takes her breaks very seriously indeed, let's start again, shall we" the she devils voice cut through his anxiety, but increased the blood flow. "I'm Missy Death Breath, and this is Super Goody Two Shoes, now Goody, behave nicely with our lovely guests please".

Ultimate broke out of his revere and spoke "Oh I'm Mr Ultimate Evil, but you can call me Ult, if you like, and this is my nemesis Super Nice Guy, we're on a break to... from a fight to the death... got a bit puffed...came in for a drink.. You know...and we mean you no harm, just being friendly like..." Ultimate looked like a little boy lost. Nice thought he's really besotted with Goody two shoes, poor fellow.

"Oh Fuck" exclaimed Goody two shoes. "Oh shit, should have known, why the fuck did we not go into that other bar. A gay bar for fuck sake, not going to get fucked in a gay bar I said. Spend fucking months being oh so fucking virtuous, defending fucking decency, fighting lustful evil, fucking 24/7, in all fucking weathers, all fucking seasons, no fucking fun, and the first break I get, a fucking drop dead gorgeous demon just wants to be fucking friendly"

While Goody was spouting Nice was staring lustily at Missy, using his X-Ray eyes, shallow rating. Missy went bright red "Please stop that" before she bit hear lip then pouted.

"Sorry...Sorry" gushed both lads. A stunned Ultimate added "You really want sex... with me...you want me...

Good v Evil

Sorry I'm not used to girls actually wanting it, usually they scream and before I get close Nice hits me... hard"

"Well, I think he's going to be occupied for a while, and I won't be the one screaming, unless it's for fucking more" Ultimate looked to Nice for help, but he was already being eaten alive by the she devil.

"I think we should move to the rooms they have at the back for just this purpose, move those two as well" said Goody taking command of the situation.

"Look I'm a bit concerned for him, he's a virgin, you know, and..."

"So's she".

"You what, surely not..."

"They will be grand, but you better be fucking good, or Goody Two Shoes will fucking eat you alive"

"You sure you don't want your parents approval first".

"Dad's dead, and not letting my fucking bitch of a fucking mother fuck you before me".

"Em.. just one question before... you know...what will you be like when you're not on a break".

"I'll scream very fucking loud, and struggle, so I hope you got a very private sound proof room".

Good v Evil

With that, I think it prudent to leave this foursome to their pleasures, after all – it's their break time, and we shouldn't be snooping, but some weeks later...

Looking down upon a filthy back alley somewhere in a teaming city, once again we observe the eternal struggle between good and evil.

Biff... Baff... Boff.

"Hold on a mo, there Ult".

"What you puffed already, not hung over again, Missy leading you astray".

"No...No... just want to talk".

"Talk?... You?... You alright, not sickening are you?"

"No, I've been thinking".

"What, and me thinking it was my blows actually giving you that pained expression".

"Oh shut up Ult, it's about me and Missy".

"On no you're not breaking up are you, Goody will be gutted".

"No.no... You and Goody still seeing each other then".

"Why would you think otherwise Nice?"

"Em...The screams, and shouted obscenities heard from your place".

Good v Evil

"You been peeping again, I told you before to stop that. Anyway – No – Goody loves that sort of thing. Cause I did have trouble at first with her language, but it's really worth putting up with... really worth it" Ultimates face went all dreamy for a moment.

"Oh good, only me and Missy were wondering if you would come to our wedding... as best man and maid of honour".

"Oh, of course – be delighted... No honoured, to be best man... And... And Goody...yes... yes ,no problem".

"Oh good, that's a relief".

"Oh. Em, church wedding? Missy in White?" asked Ultimate.

"Em, no, not under the circumstances"

"What? Her being Evil like" Ult laughed.

"No... Her being pregnant..."

"What..." It took a few moments for that to sink in. "You old dog you...Well, well, well!" he paused "Oh I'm not sure how Goody will take that one, they are locked in a fight to the death, just like us, but I'm sure she'll be delighted".

"Ult, I've been thinking. About this fight to the death thing?"

"WHAT?"

You Can't Ask for Coffee

Can't ask for coffee in a coffee shop no more
That word disappears once you're in the door

There's a bountiful list stuck up on the wall
With strange brews – so you start to feel a fool

A Barista comes to serve, but not with a writ
What do you ask for to get your caffeine hit?

Do you stick by your guns, stand tall, go for "coffee"
And see their look like I'd just fell out the tree

Do you chicken out, play it safe, ask for "Tea"
But can you cope with "What speciality

Or do you take a stab and pick at random
Fingers crossed, and pay a king's ransom

Hope the question of the options would stop
Hope it don't have a straw or stuff floating on top

Oh God! Now you're asked the question of size
Manliness demands you're a large- but it's lies

Then finally you find out how wrong you got it
When you're asked, "you want cinnamon on it".

"Shush"

"Shush"

"Shush, did you hear that"

"I didn't hear anything, John"

"You must have, listen George"

George cocked his head to the side and did as he was asked.

"Do you hear it, George" asked his impatient companion.

"What, all I can hear is your jabbering... And fidgeting" snapped George.

"OK sorry, I'll shut up, but will you listen, please George" pleaded John.

"OK, OK, I'll listen"

Only a few seconds passed before John could not wait any longer.

"Well?"

"Give us a chance mate, anyway, what for heaven's sake am I supposed to be listening for" George was getting irritated with his best friend.

"A sound..."

"Of course a sound, John, what sort?"

"Don't snap at me, please George, you know my nerves are shot"

"Shush"

"Sorry John, but that's why I brought you up here, can't you just relax and enjoy the view"

"The sound George, like a snake, but quiet like"

"A bloody snake, John. We're still in Ireland you know" George regretted saying it immediately. He didn't wish to upset the man any more.

"Sorry John... You going to be still, and quiet yourself, John"

John just nodded. Then George tried again for what seemed like an age, but in truth was but a few seconds.

Then George said "Look John, I can only hear the wind up here"

John did a little nervous jiggle, and said "It's definitely there, I hear it , I know it's there" There was a little desperation in his voice.

"John you're getting paranoid, have you taken your pills this morning?"

"Of course, I have, George...I think!" A look of doubt crossed his face for a moment.

"Well, take a chill pill now, you're spoiling the view" George couldn't help himself; he never could deal sympathetically with his friends nervous condition. He cursed himself under his breath.

"Shush"

"No George, I hear it, it's getting closer, louder, you must hear it now, please George" John's tone of voice was now sounding more determined, and urgent.

George tutted in annoyance. He cursed John for his fears of snakes, spiders, and anything else that move of its own volition, but strangely - not heights. He reluctantly stopped admiring the panoramic views, took a deep breath of the fresh air. "Ok John" he said and started looking around them, and then he looked up. Johns' eyes nervous followed Georges' gaze.

"What the fuck!" cried George

"The balloons ripped".

There Ain't No Bleedin' Justice

There Ain't No Bleedin' Justice

There ain't no bleeding justice, that's what I say, and it bloody well rained!

The day I'd looked forward to, and dreaded in equal measure....And it pissed out of the heavens!

It was my last day at that bleeding factory, after 50 wasted years, and it was a misery. The rain was the best bit. There was a bleeding party, for pity's sake! A celebration for the departure of the longest ever serving employee, so they said. Me! The only worker they ever had; not to be killed by toxic fumes, malfunctioning machinery, carelessness, or foul play. The only one to not succumb to crippling injury, chronic disease, incensed wives, or plain madness. The only one to survive the scrapheap of the multiple culls caused by 'economics' to reach the retirement age and still turn up to be paid.

The previous month had been the worst of my life, and that's saying something. When I joined the company, life was simple. You knew were you stood, up to the knees in the muck mostly. The town had one main employer, the factory, and it was massive then. Since my education was a lost cause, my only choice, apart from outright criminality, was to work on the factory floor. At the time it was considered a secure job, but for me it was a life sentence. The company cared little for its work force, and we cared little, sorry, nothing for

There Ain't No Bleedin' Justice

it. No Health and safety, no Human Resources department, no pension plans, no prospect of leaving the factory floor. Just the way I liked it, simple.

But these days! Bloody hell, they tried to send me on pre-retirement courses paid for by the company, expenses and all. Questioned me about whether I'd provided myself with a big enough pension pot to live on. I was given endless advice on grants, and allowances, that I could apply for. I fobbed them off by telling them I had a sort of private pension sorted. What kind, I was asked. I said 'private', bloody nosey parkers.

All this caring, what's that all about, what's in it for them? Don't tell me they've grown a conscience, don't give me that, they're after something, I know.

Anyway, I went in to work on that day out of habit, and despite my best efforts was not allowed to miss the party. They laid on food and drink, sort of. "Pretty fours", chinky finger food, and crust less sambos, even had vegan options! And Drink, seems these new Asian owners, were teatotal, so, no booze, soft drinks only, for bloody hell's sake. Still, my dad's lesson taught me well – a hip flask in each jacket pocket would numb the agony somewhat. That's the only lesson my dad taught me. He beat it into me if he ever made it home from the pub still able to speak. It was trust no one.

There Ain't No Bleedin' Justice

Look after number one. Don't rely on others; they'll eventually let you down. A lesson he would occasionally reinforce by never fulfilling the rare promises he made to me.

All the chit-chat, and more questions about my future, suggestions to join this group or that, so that I wouldn't get lonely since the wife has gone, and what with no family. The torture seemed to go on for ages, I didn't think it could get any worse, but then came the speeches! The HR manager gave a speech, what a nightmare. They did their research about my history in the place; I'll say that for them. The interminable driveller dug up old memories, some good, but many bad. He spoke of me and 3 other lads who joined on the same day as me, called us the four musketeers, inseparable rouges. Tom, Dick, Harry, and me.

He brought up my losing both parents at a young age, and he went on about how sad it was that I was the only survivor of the gang. He catalogued their demise, then went on to the missus, a long term factory girl herself, and how sad and mysterious her disappearance was, the bastard, what the fuck did he know? My day grew darker, but I grinned and bared it all till the end, and I took my leave, clutching the envelope holding the collection they had made for me, a total of just over 1 quid for each year of my life. No

There Ain't No Bleedin' Justice

crap gold watch, just handshake with the little china men, and it was over.

I walked away, plodded the long plod home, to that house I called home. That house that was my so called parents' house, and now was mine, by rights, earned rights. The parents had actually owned it outright, no idea how that happened, and I don't want to know. The decor and the furniture, and, all the tacky ornaments were the wife's'. All of it, reminders of the past. A past I'm done with. Screw the past.

I plonked my arse in her bloody uncomfortable sofa. She bought the stupid thing cos it looked posh. Bloody Woman. I sat amongst the piles of rubbish (at least that was mine) and remembered.

I remembered the end of my childhood. When I reached the grand old age of 15 both my parents died. My Dad fell down the stairs in a drunken stupor, and got his head smashed in. That was shortly after Mum had told me that my Dad wasn't actually my dad. On hearing this revelation I immediately presumed that she meant that she was a slag, and was at it with every layabout in the town, while 'dad' was out at work earning his drinking money. Stood to reason, how else could we afford to eat? But no! – She said I was adopted... That shook me rigid. What fool would let a violent drunk and a prostitute adopt? Course, she

There Ain't No Bleedin' Justice

claimed things had been different then, 'dad' wasn't always drunk in those days, and was far more attentive to her needs. So why the need to adopt, I probed. Well, she said she didn't want to go through all that pregnancy/birth stuff was far too messy and painful for her to be bothered with. I continued my questioning with would this birthing lark be more or less painful than the beatings she gets most nights when her husband gets kicked out of the pub. "Ah" she replied, "the bottle of gin I drinks before he gets home softens the blows". I remonstrated with her that he only beats her because she never has his dinner ready for him when he gets in because she's too drunk, and he only stays in the pub and drinks more because he comes home to a drunk every night. To which all she said was she hates cooking.

Anyway, she was found the following morning - beaten to death. The weapon used in this violent attack was deemed to be her husband's stout stick, which he normally kept under the stairs. This cudgel had been used in many beatings before, but never with such venom. It was found at the bottom of the stairs by the prostrate body of her husband. I was found hiding in my bedroom, splattered with blood, in an apparent state of shock at the deaths, and in fear of my life from the violence of my 'dad'. In truth it was more to do with the number of times I had to drop Granny's metal weight on his head after he survived being pushed

There Ain't No Bleedin' Justice

down the stairs. The fear I felt was that I might not be believed innocent, but I needn't have worried, the dad's violence was well known to the investigating detective, as well as my mums' bed. He also had a soft spot for me, mum probably never told him I was adopted, may have been spun a lie that he was somehow responsible for me. So he worked out that I had come down stairs on hearing the two of them rowing and dad taking up the cudgel to do for his wife once and for all. I was then running up stairs to escape my father's mad wroth when he slipped from the top of the stairs in his drunken state. Forensics wasn't a precise science in those days, and my failure to contradict the officer of the law was considered enough to wrap the case up nice and neat, and quick like – sorted.

I not being considered adult was to go into care, but the same detective offered me a place in his home. He and his wife never managed to create children, him being working all the time and visiting my mum the rest, when he wasn't drinking. I accepted the offer, after I met his wife, a lovely and caring lady. I accepted her affections too, as I managed to put into practice all the activity I observed through my peep hole into my parents bedroom, when dad wasn't there. It worked quite well for a while, until the detective applied his talents to his home life, and I escaped out of harm's way. By this time I'd reached adulthood, left school,

There Ain't No Bleedin' Justice

retook possession of the parents place, and joined the factory. Before he could get at me, the detective was arrested for what he did to his wife, which was what he'd threatened to do to me. Fortunately for me, while he was in prison awaiting trial, a number of cons he had framed years back got their own back on him, which was a bit stupid, because they got life for it.

Anyway, my thoughts then travelled forward to Tom, Dick, and Harry. It's true, we were inseparable once we left school, and joined the firm. We did everything together, including girls, if we could, and never got caught.

In our early years in the factory, I saw the odd retirement, old 'lifers' getting thrown on the scrap heap. They only got a gold watch if they were lucky. What was the point of that? Now that they didn't have to get up in the mornings no more, what's giving them a watch for? Was it just to let them know how much time they wasted working for the factory? Was it too count the minutes of their wife's nagging? Course the watch would be taken straight to the pawn shop to get only just enough money for one week's booze. We hear of their deaths within a couple of years of 24/7 exposure to their wife's nagging. The gold watch would then find its way back to the factory in time to be presented to the next lucky recipient.

There Ain't No Bleedin' Justice

It was then I decided that I should be looking after my retirement. The lads thought I was mad. We were still in our early twenties then, but I persevered, and convinced them. Of course, I wasn't talking of giving up my hard-earned cash to some pension company who would squirrel it away to pay their executives expenses, and then fob us off with some pittance on my retirement. Oh no. I had in mind a real pension pot. A pension that required no cash outlay, and had nobody creaming off a share. We just nick stuff from the factory. I had it all worked out, fool proof. It was so simple, my plan would involve nothing large, just small but regular amounts that would build into a tidy sum, tax free, and nobody would know, guaranteed.

And it worked; slowly we built up a handsome retirement fund. Part of my plan was that we should tell no one else of this little project, just the four of us. No one, not Father, Mother, Sister, Brother, friend, girlfriend, or worse, a wife, of the existence of this fund. It would be our secret, to be split on retirement, and not a moment before. Couldn't have anybody wondering how we could afford stuff, bringing attention on ourselves, all those curtain twitchers, nosey bastards. I knew I was wrong to trust them all, after my dad's lesson – trust no one, they will only let you down, and they did.

There Ain't No Bleedin' Justice

Tom started it. Got married, the stupid arse. Got one of the factory girls up the duff, and "fell in love". Fell in to a tar pit more like, swallowed him whole.

The other two lads shared their concern with me, but they didn't have the same level of conviction about it as I did, so Tom was just given a stiff talking too about the rules of the pension pot. It didn't work, Toms new missus was demanding improvements in his financial position. Tom melted and told the greedy bitch about the pot. So now she knew our secrets, and started making demands, she wanted money now. Me and Dick were in agreement. A big fat "No", but Harry didn't back us up. He was falling into the same hole as Tom; a girl had got her hands round his wallet, having already had a firm grip on another part of his non-removable anatomy. He started on about us being unambitious, we could increase our little business without trouble, and… and (this is a biggy) reinvest in other areas. By that he was inferring moving into illicit substances. It seems he, meaning his girlfriend, had the right contacts. "We could make a fortune" We, that is Me and Dick, were accused for being scared, stick in the muds, would never amount to much.

We voted on Harry's idea. Two all. But then Tom's wife demanded a vote to make it 3-2 in favour of branching out. The meeting ended in a flaming row. Tom and Harry wanted their share and were going to go it alone.

There Ain't No Bleedin' Justice

It was a relief that they, at least, had the integrity for not allowing Tom's missus the vote.

The accident that did for Tom and his wife was a nasty one. Nice funeral though.

Harry went very quiet on us after that, he seemed somewhat troubled. Dick asked if he still wanted his share, but he just shook his head, and walked away.

Now that we were down to three partners, Dick was getting a bit confused. He was the worst of us at sums. He could only manage half fractions. To work out his share of the pot, when we were four, he would divide the total by two, then two again for his share. Now without Tom, the pot was to be divided by three, he was totally flummoxed. He didn't like not knowing, so he was forever asking me to work it out for him. He was starting to get on my nerves.

After a while Harry started talking again, though he seemed very weary of us, god knows why.

At lunch, one day, he started on about Tom's poor old mother being left penniless. Me and Dick exchanged looks. We guessed what was coming, give Tom's share to his old mum, anonymous like. Dick pipped up "We'll think about it, Harry". It seemed to settle Harry a bit. I told Dick once we were alone, that I didn't like this turn of events, and he just nodded.

There Ain't No Bleedin' Justice

They found Harry hanging by the neck in his lodgings. There was a note, just said "sorry". The word was he had gambling debts, owed his mates money, and him and his bird had got involved in drugs. At least that's what me and Dick told the cops, we, being his closest mates, like! The raid the cops did on the girlfriend's place turned up enough dirty drugs to put her away for a long time. That caused me to question Dick as to how, but seems he knew a bent cop who owed him a favour. I was impressed, but a little concerned by this development.

Dick seemed a lot happier, less furrows on his forehead when working out his share. Also our shares had doubled in size from when we were four. He only needed to halve once, still a struggle for him, but he could manage.

It was then that Gladys got her claws into me. Another bleeding factory girl. Seems she wore out all the rest of the lads. Dick was her previous victim. Sucked him dry, in more ways than one, then latched on to me, like a limpet.

Now it was Dick's turn to be unimpressed by the development. He gave me a stern warning that she was not to be trusted. He had thought she had an idea about our scam, and maybe other things too. He'd probably blurted it to her, but denied he had, claimed

There Ain't No Bleedin' Justice

she had been friendly with Tom's wife. I wasn't so sure.

It started to occur to me, that Dick might be getting the idea that he wouldn't have to halve the pot at all if I wasn't around. He had accused me of trying to cheat him, when I worked out his share when we were three. Now and again I'd catch him staring at me funny like, sizing me up. Giving me the willies, it was. Gladys probably put that thought in his dumb head.

Dick's funeral was a small affair, just me, Gladys, and a representative of the company. The latter was still insisting that Dick's machine did not malfunction. I had to tell the new Health and Safety wallers that Dick was always ignoring the safety rules, and there was his drinking! Oh! And after that warning signs were put up everywhere. So Dick got the blame. Misadventure was the verdict. But Gladys had other ideas, so we got married. I had no choice.

Still, she was a good cook, and was well practiced in other areas of married life. So for some time things settled down and the pension pot grew.

But then Gladys wanted things now, like foreign holidays, and fancy stuff. Sun Holidays had started to come in packets. Soon we were boarding planes for the sun. She was in her element, but I hated them, couldn't get decent food, but at least the drinks were

There Ain't No Bleedin' Justice

cheap. Before I knew it, part of the pot was "invested" in a luxury villa in the south of Spain. Gladys being quite clever had worked it all out herself, I mean, the pot, and the lads. I think she had an idea about my parents too.

As time went by her demands on me grew, and she would travel to the villa three times a year. We told all and sundry she was gone to look after her poor old mum, up the country, just so no questions would be raised about how we afforded the flights. We didn't tell anyone that we had put the old dear in the ground the previous year. Well, it was a mercy really; nursing homes are so expensive, cost an arm and a leg.

Her spending was starting to get out of control, and I was starting to suspect she had a fancy man at the villa. So, she disappeared. Didn't come back from one of her trips to the villa. I had to play the innocent jilted husband, with no idea about her frequent trips aboard. The cops were suspicious at first, after all I'd just relayed the patio. They were none too pleased to find just the missus dead cat under it. I'd always hated that cat. Turned out she was "seeing" some criminal type out there, a nasty piece of work. I'd had some dealings with him when I was at the villa, a man unpopular with other criminal elements in the same area. Bringing the attention of the British cops to their playground was not making him a popular boy, even though he had

There Ain't No Bleedin' Justice

nothing to do with it. It wasn't long before he disappeared too, cause now I owed some equally nasty guys a favour. I never wanted the villa anyway, so good riddance to it. The cops gave up looking after a while, although I don't think they were ever convinced by my story. I'm thankful I got hold of false passports for us to use when both of us went to Spain. She of course wouldn't use hers on her extra trips, never copped on as to why I used one. See, the cops had no proof I left old blighty, and followed her on that last flight.

And now I sit in this god-awful chair, staring at the walls, alone. No dinners cooked, place is a mess, no laundry done, bed sheets stink. What now?

The pot had been raided many times over to assuage the missus' greed, but there was still enough to provide a few comforts, like alcohol, to numb the pain. I was beginning to understand people like those I referred to as my mum and dad. At least I never had a kid to do me in. I was my own boss, but the thought depressed me. I got nobody to blame but me.

After a while of this soul searching, I was disturbed by an unwanted knock at the door. I knew that knock. No, it wasn't the long arm of the law, no. It was one of the local factory widows. Since the wife's absence, a few of the lonely ones, who never became propertied,

There Ain't No Bleedin' Justice

started turning their attention towards me. A widower with property, and some seemed to think a handsome pension pot, was a desirable commodity to these old dears.

That made up my mind; I nipped out the back door and scarpered off to the cop shop. Once there, I explained that I wanted to confess to all my crimes. Well, you'd think Christmas had come early and the cops had granted every wish they ever had. I was invited in to a little private office, offered tea or coffee, and even a fag. I was treated like a long-lost friend, and they gleefully took notes of all I confessed too. I confessed to my so-called parents' death first. Then said I framed that detective for the beating of his wife (well she did like her sex rough, I just over did it a bit). I admitted to defrauding the factory for nearly 50 years. Took full responsibility for the demise of my three mates, and their girls. At that point I asked if that was enough to lock me away for the rest of my life... Free bed and board, no females, no one to trust, a simple life. The officers were a bit non-committal about sentence length, so I told them in which room to lift the floor boards to find the missus. Out of principle, I only confessed to an 'aid and abet' on Gladys's mother, after all it was her idea. But just for good measure, and to be sure, I offered to take on a few unsolved rape cases that me and the lads may have had a hand, or more, in, back in the day. That should do it, they all

There Ain't No Bleedin' Justice

agreed. It was happiness all round. They said they just needed to get my DNA into a bit of evidence, and bobs your uncle; I'll be stitched up for life.

Bastards, damn them, I trusted someone again. Put my future into some else's hands and got cheated. One of the rape cases was an under-age job. Got me labelled a paedophile, the bastards. Now I'm locked up with a load of purves, and I've to watch my back every minute, of every day. This is a nightmare.

There ain't no bleeding justice in this world.

Words I should Have Said

The words rang round and round my head
Words that really should have been said
But my tongue remained still instead
Now my future hangs by a thread

I should have spoken truth out loud
Should have shouted to the whole crowd
But there I sat, and silently howled
Cowardly sat with my head bowed

Those words would have cured all my ills
Now I'm swallowing a bitter pill
And she's giving me looks that'll kill
Plus, now I'm left to pay the bill

I should have had better foresight
Wanted to say, try as I might
My better judgement lost the fight
And my mouth remained fast shut tight

Words that declared how much i cared
Words that I really should have shared
Thoughts that I should have dared
But in truth I was just too scared

Those words that rung around my mind
Those words if said so cruel yet kind
That even if that dress was designed
It wasn't for someone with your behind

Do You Love Me?

Do You Love Me?

A single bedside lamp, barely bright enough to read by, was the only light in the room. Brian stood at the curtained window. He could be in his thirties, balding and plump, but in the light it was hard to tell. He certainly did not look like he got out much – dressed to thrill for the 1980's – Did not look the type to do well with the ladies, either – but he's not alone in the room, Gerri was sitting in an unlit corner.

"Do you love me?" said a weak voice.

"Oh, don't start that again, Gerri!" Brian replied truculently.

"DO. YOU. LOVE ME?" still weak – but with some intent.

"Of course I do, you know I do".

"Then say it".

"Oh come on girl, I provide you with every comfort, keep you fed, watered, what more proof could you ask for".

"SAY IT".

"Ok, Ok… I Love You. OK now".

"Then let me go".

"NO".

Do You Love Me?

"If you truly love me, you'd let me go".

"NO, it's too dangerous. Can't let you go out there" he waved vaguely at the window.

"You don't truly love me then - just want to possess me".

"That's not true, you're special, I'd do anything for you...You know that. The world out there is crawling with predators round every corner, just waiting to do you harm. I'll do anything you ask, but not that; I've got to keep you safe".

"Did you tell all the others that too?"

"No, no, they meant nothing to me, I swear".

"But you still kept them, didn't you?"

"Well yes, but not here. They were never in my room. I never loved them, only you".

"You've only brought me in here since your mothers gone. She wouldn't let you, She didn't approve, did she?"
"You leave Mother out of this, don't you talk about her".

"Did you let them go, tell me the truth; I know when you're lying".

"They're all gone now, so you can stop talking about them – they're gone".

Do You Love Me?

"Didn't let any of them go did you?... killed the lot didn't you".

"No, no, that's not true. Some got sick. It's true - I put them out of their misery. I'm not a monster".

"Oh aren't you? You didn't let that one, what you call her 'Charlotte'; you didn't let her go, did you. She made too much noise, didn't she, so you chopped her up, cooked, and fed her to your mother".

"She had it coming, the bitch, never gave me any peace".

"Charlotte, or your mother – both, I reckon".

"I told you not to talk about Mother, after what you did".

"I did nothing; it was you that fed her the poisoned meat. I was locked up in the basement all the time".

"It wasn't poisoned – it was just a bit off – I had no room in the freezer for the bitch. You told me to give it to her, it was your idea. You always hated Mother".

"Oh, don't give me that – she made your life a misery – you're the one that wanted her dead".

"No, no stop taunting me like that. I loved Mother".

"She drove you mad; kept you a prisoner, just like you do to us".

Do You Love Me?

"Stop it, stop it".

"Then let me go".

"NO,NO,NO".

"Just let me into the garden, let me see the sky".

"NO – they will see you".

"You let one of us go into the garden – when your mother was at the Bingo - was she your real favourite".

"No – I didn't – you're mistaken".
"Mistaken – don't think so – heard you talking to 'Betsy' was it – don't lie to me – you know I can tell".

"No... Well – she was sick – I let her get some air – didn't work though".

"You could have called someone – to help her".

"What – I couldn't do that – couldn't risk it – they've got eyes everywhere"

"You are a monster".

"Don't talk like that – I rescued you all".

"Could you, at least, open the curtains for a while – let some light in".

Do You Love Me?

"Can't…They might see you – can't have that".

Gerri was silent for a moment, then said *"If the others have all gone, why do you still go down the basement? And so often too".*

"I don't… well I got tools and stuff down there".

"And you talk to your tools do you, and they scream, and shout back – do they".

"OK, look, I can't just let them go, and I…"

"Do you enjoy their company, do you touch them, and caress them, like you do me".

"It's…It's not the same, I tell you. It's not the same".

"Yet you do – don't you, don't lie, I know your inner most thoughts – you can't hide them from me".

"Look, you're not like the others, they don't talk to me, I can't have a conversation with them. They don't understand…I've kept them safe…Safe from those men that did those things… unspeakable things to you, to you all."

"Safe…Safe? You kept us locked up, in that dark… dank and dismal hole".

"Mother wouldn't have understood – she'd have told the police – I wouldn't be able to keep you, safe".

Do You Love Me?

"Your mothers gone now – she's dead – So what's stopping you bringing them up now"?

"They could be seen – they could get out – those men could find them again".

"Why you so sure about those men – why would they have any idea where we are – how could they know"?

"Don't know – but they are here. Lurking down the street, waiting in unmarked cars, I've seen them".

"Your imagining it – getting paranoid – keeping us all locked up – It's doing your head in – maybe it's time to give it up".

"Stop it... Stop it – I know your game – trying to drive me mad – being my conscience. Just shut it – or back down the hole you'll go, my lady".

"What – and you all alone up here rambling about in this big empty house with no one to talk too".

"I go out, I go to work, I talk to people".

"Oh yeh – do you want fries with that – great conversationalist – you"

"What would you know…."

"You haven't even told anybody about your mother yet – have you".

Do You Love Me?

"I told you not to mention Mother again – I told you".

"Someone's going to ask where she is before too long – I heard you digging in the garden after she died – is that what you did with the body – buried along with Betsy and all the rest".

"You… You… keep your mouth shut – get out of my head".

"You've buried her in the garden – you can't lie to me – If it was an accident why didn't you tell anyone about her death".

"Couldn't– I'll lose the house, it's left to a cats home - they won't understand – I had no choice".

"You need help".

"I can manage – thank you".

"No – you need help – professional help – you know what I mean".

"What – you mean those men in the white coats – I'm not mad".

"You sure about that – you're the one talking with an rat in a cage after all"

"But you are a talking rat – a Lab rat – I rescued you from that evil place, you've a speaker box round your neck – and all the operations on your brain…"

Do You Love Me?

"You try telling that to the men in the white coats when they come for you".

"What do you mean – coming for me? You talk to me!"

"Do I – really – do I – got any recordings of our little chit-chats? If I could talk, would the lab want to show me off – wouldn't I be famous, be on TV, have my own chat show, ah? Then there's adverts – Guinea Pigs watching humans for an electricity company, I would be like them".

"They're not real – it's fake, it's all fake".

"Exactly- So who's going to believe you – a 30 year old boy who killed and buried his mother?"

"Don't you dare start that – I liberated you from that horrible place where they stuck you full of drugs, and did terrible experiments on you – did ghastly things to your mind – you told me?"

"Who started talking first?"

"Well I did, I suppose, just trying to calm you down during the escape – look – is this all cause you miss your friends – I could get you a mate – you could start a family – would you like that?"

"What? I'm a bloody thinking, talking being – think I'd want a mate who wouldn't understand a single word – who would just want to eat, shit, hump, and sleep all

Do You Love Me?

day and night! I'm a freak – a mad scientist's creation. When you broke in, you told us we'd be famous on T.V. I co-operated cause you'd make me a film star celebrity – YOU LIED".

"I didn't mean it like that – I didn't know you could talk – I meant the release would be on the news and your pictures would go viral. People would love you – give you caring homes"

"As a pet"

"Yes a pet – I didn't know"

"But they was no press release – was there"

"It wasn't safe – the Lab kept quiet – no one knew the raid happened at all"

"Yet again – nothing to back you up – Animals don't talk"

"No – don't do this".

"Animals don't talk, ask anybody- you haven't showed me to anybody, and nobody else has heard me. It's all in your mind, now you've killed your mother – you've gone totally mad. All alone in this big house".

"Don't say that – Mother was an accident – I never knew she'd react to dog meat like that... but you knew didn't you?"

Do You Love Me?

"It was you all along – you made me do it – Mother hated you from the moment I brought you home, she wanted me to get you put down – she thought you looked evil".

"Let me go, if you don't like what I tell you – if you can't accept the truth – or those men in white coats will be coming for you for sure, just let me out of the cage – let me stretch my legs a bit"".

"It was you – last time I let you out – found you sitting on my phone – you'd dialled somebody – hadn't you – thought I'd heard a voice on the phone – you were trying to get me fitted up for Mothers murder - weren't you?"

"I am saying nothing more – after all I'm just a pet".

Brian swung round from the window and marched to the corner where the cage was sitting, opened the door and reached in.

"Come here you evil bitch – your cage don't protect you from me – ah got you – ouch... You bit me, you … you bitch."

He let go, and the rat was out of the cage and slipped under the bed.

"Bugger! Damn it! I'm bleeding. Right I'm going to deal with this, and when I come back… you'll better be back in the cage, or you're going down the hole for a while –

Do You Love Me?

I'll stick you in with Igor – he'll teach you some manners my girl".

SLAM, footsteps fading

Scrabbling noise, tap,taping Ring ring, Ring ring, click

"Hallo, Professor Gluckfussor here, who am I speaking to".

"Hi, Professor, it's GERRI, look, I'm really sorry about escaping. You were right; it's not good out here for a talking rat. I'm ready to come back in, so get your men to 13 The Avenue. This guy's mad –he thinks I'm female! It's getting out of hand here. My batteries low – if I stop talking he'll put me in with that mad rat Igor - the sad bastard will tear me apart, Please come quick. If Brian discovers I'd pissed in his mothers' food he'll kill me for sure".

"I'm sorry, you'll have to speak up – too faint – my hearing isn't what it used to be, I don't have my little friend to help me – he run away you know - speak up"

"Professor it's me……."

"Oh dear – I think I got a heavy breather – go away" the line goes dead.

Gluckfussors'.**E**xperimental.**R**esearch.**R**at.   no   **1** screamed, as only rats can.

Midnight, on the Dot

Midnight on the Dot

I don't know when it started, and I don't know of any reason why it should have happened. At first I thought it was just dreaming, sleepwalking, or some such. NO! Correction, at first I didn't realise it was actually happening. After all, who would? "The Dark Hour" for heaven's sake, an hour after midnight that only I could experience...While the rest of the world slept... madness, unbelievable wouldn't you think?

The first time that I became aware of something...out of the ordinary was, I think, back in August...Or September. I had gone to bed before 11pm, as usual, Jean (the wife) didn't like the idea of late nights. I woke, and glanced at the clock (It's one of those digital jobbies). Midnight, on the dot. I cursed, most likely, and turned over ever so slowly, so as not to disturb the wife, her being a terrible light sleeper, closed the eyes and tried to go back to sleep. Sleep wouldn't come, something didn't feel right. After a while of trying to ignore the feeling, I turned back over, to try again. Just before I closed my eyes I caught sight of the clock. Midnight, on the dot.

WTF! ... Dreaming, that's it. Dreamt I had been awake. Weird or what? Calmed by the thought, I drifted back off to sleep.

Midnight on the Dot

By morning, I'd forgotten the incident, but it happened every now and again, would wake at midnight... With the same 'dream'!

I had thought of telling Jean about my 'recurring dream' but she's a Psychiatrist! Probably have me labelled straight away, as suffering from some mental illness. Have me fitted for a straight jacket; she already thinks (Sorry – knows) I'm a basket case. I had to be, to marry her, my own shrink. It would just be another thing to ridicule me in front of her friends – 'The Coven' I called them. They spent their time bemoaning their husbands as the most stupid, lazy, pathetic, creatures ever created by God (Good Christians every one of them) For them divorce was out of the question, unless there was money in it, and another fool available to make their lives hell. (Read that last bit whichever way you like)

Anyway... Where was I... Oh yes. I finally realised something really weird was happening on, about, the fourth, or maybe fifth time. We had been out for a meal – her works do – I ate far more than was good for me. Jean would not allow me to drink alcohol in public, so I had to do something to pass the time. So I woke, glanced at clock. Midnight, on the dot. 'AGAIN'!

I rose, quicker than I would have liked, due to the severity of my stomach cramps, and hobbled to the en-

Midnight on the Dot

suite, clumsily shutting the door, and dropping shorts in the nick of time. I took quite a while, or so I thought, before feeling safe to raise myself from the seat. Another stab of cramp and I was on the throne again, for another dose. Eventually, when satisfied there was no more to come, and I couldn't put off facing the witch any longer, I cleaned, flushed, and prepared to face the music. In the past I had tried not flushing, not washing in the faint hope that it wouldn't wake her, but that only sharpened her tongue, and steeled her glare.

I sheepishly opened the door. Surprise! I wasn't blinded by the light, nor her glare. She was still asleep. Wonders would never cease. I gave an internal 'Yippee' and climbed back into bed, extra gingerly. 'Let's not spoil a good thing'.

Then, just before I shut my eyes I saw the time. Midnight, on the dot! NO! Now I was wide awake, and sat up, without thinking. Bloody clock bloody broken! Other thoughts hit me. Jean not only was still asleep, she was not moving. She hadn't moved a muscle, from my rising till then, and also was quiet – deathly so. She never slept still, went on walking holidays in her sleep. I told her once. I was wrong again, of course. We had a king size bed, of which she required three-quarters of it, leaving me clinging on to the edge some nights. She was never silent either, snoring, snorting, or mumbling, not loudly, but just enough to be disturbing

Midnight on the Dot

(when I could hear the words). Silence...Stillness... That was the strangeness I had felt. WTF! I thought about touching her, to see if she was cold...But chickened, it's bad enough waking her, but touching in bed! I lay back down, shut my eyes, and drifted off into a fitful sleep, and dreamt of Jean being dead, after I strangled her in my sleep. I slept well that night.

Morning came, Jean rose like the Kraken, and the previous night events sunk back into the mists of time.

At coffee break the following day it all came back to me. No matter how I tried, I could not make any sense of it. The alarm had gone off at the allotted time – so the clock was not broken. As I said, the wife always wakes if I get up, the previous night was the first time ever that she didn't. Maybe I've never woken at that time before – maybe it's safe to get up when she's been asleep for only an hour. Maybe.

I resolved that next time, if there was one, I would watch her for a while.

Didn't have to wait long, the following night I woke at... guess what... Midnight, on the dot, but had forgotten my resolution. I turned over, tried to sleep, for a while. Then remembered, and sat up quickly, with a sudden fleeting regret, the jolt would surely wake her, then have to face the interrogation as to why I woke her. Honesty would have got me locked up. No! She didn't

Midnight on the Dot

budge. No sound, no movement, but I was still unable to bring myself to touch her. The coward, that I am, resolved to investigate the time problem instead.

I rose and went to the dressing table, and picked up my watch. It was stuck on Midnight just like the clock. On closer inspection I could see the second hand quivering, trying to move with each second, but failing. I now had 3 odd things to consider, the clock, my watch, and sleeping beauty. What else? I ventured downstairs. The TV - that will settle it. It took a while to find the hidden remote. Once found I turned on and started flicking through the channels. All the same – a different still picture on each of them. Clocks – TV clock, mantelpiece clock, kitchen clock, cooker...All – Midnight on the dot. WTF. I must be dreaming. This can't be real. I pinched myself expecting no pain, but it hurt. I needed a drink, so headed for my hidden store. I poured a stiff Whiskey, and drained it in one go. The drink resolved nothing, so I returned to the bedroom. Wake her I thought, show her, and prove I'm not going mad!

That resolve disappeared the moment I got close to her. She was not moving, no sign of breathing, or any rise and fall of her chest. She was facing my side of the bed, so I got back under the covers... In case she woke. I got closer to her. No breath...She's not breathing! WTF! No... Yes...No breath...She's dead? A

Midnight on the Dot

little involuntary evil thought crept into my head. 'Ding, Dong, the witch is dead... A thought I quickly suppressed, and backed away from her. A small tingle of guilt ran through me, but only small. I reached out to touch her to see if she was cold. 'Ding dong...' stop it, I told myself. Before I could make contact, with my finger an inch from her nose, I heard a click from the clock, and Jean let out a big snort, a sudden intake of breath, and then settled into her slightly irregular rhythm of quiet snort/snoring. 'Bugger'. I withdrew my finger from the proximity of her face, turned over, and tried to go back to sleep. It took some time, I can tell you.

The next thing I knew, the alarm went off. I slammed my hand down to silence the morning traffic reports, and felt the jolt of her ladyship's hulk launching herself into the river of life, full of the joys of spring. While I suffering a pang of pain from the shifted springs of the bed. 5 minutes peace I thought. Downstairs I heard her crashing round the kitchen, as if trying to raise the dead. Then a brief, and unusual silence, followed by the thump of climbing the stairs with intent. 'Oh shit! What have I done?' sprung into my head. Her progress was slow and deliberate, that mode of approach that she used that announced 'you're in big trouble, John'.

She manifested in the doorway. "John – you've been drinking" It wasn't a question.

Midnight on the Dot

"What" my brain hadn't got into gear, I'm not a morning person.

"You've been drinking... in the night" and she held up the whiskey bottle, and dirtied glass.

"No I haven't. " For that moment, I hadn't remembered the tipple I took last night, which meant I said it with conviction.

"You have, I have the evidence" she waggled the bottle and glass at me.

"But how? You would have woken up if I'd got up; you know you're a light sleeper, God! If I turn in my sleep you give me a dig in the ribs" That was no exaggeration...except for the Dark Hour. A slight look of puzzlement crossed her face.

"Before you came to bed? She said that without much conviction.

"I was in bed before you, surely you remember that" By the look on her face that memory was clear, and was giving her some problems. At this stage I had remembered my trip downstairs, but this was too good not to play on.

"You must have got up" this was almost a plea. It was evident she had not expected any form of defence from me, and was not ready for my arguments.

Midnight on the Dot

"How could I have, dear" I was beginning to enjoy myself. It was a rare moment when I could have her doubting herself. In her mind she was never wrong where I was concerned. I'd always been in the wrong, for the last 10 years, our entire marriage. Usually the evidence didn't matter – guilty, until proven guilty, but now her own knowledge was getting in the way of her truth. The fact that I was in the wrong, just made it all the more delicious for me. I knew it wouldn't last long – her truths always outweighed the evidence in the end.

The exchange ended, she spun and thumped back down stairs then raised an even greater cacophony in the kitchen. The rest of the day continued more or less as usual, except for the extra edge in her snappiness towards me, and my slightly less depressed mood than usual.

I didn't experience The Dark Hour again until the following week, by which time my midnight drink was forgotten.

When I woke saw the clock – Midnight on the dot, my hand didn't hesitate – I reached out and touched her exposed arm – it was as warm as it ever was, to the touch, despite no sign of breathing. Then I tried to find a pulse – she had to have one I told myself, even if she was a heartless bitch. Nothing... Well... Something...very faint, but hardly a pulse. Was she in

Midnight on the Dot

a coma? –I did not know the symptoms. A thought surfaced – I could do whatever I liked to her . Sex! Whoa! No way Jose, that thought made my stomach turn . Did I really fancy her once. Once maybe, only once, then we got married!.

No forget that. Smother her... Pointless, she's hardly breathing as it is.

I then remembered the midnight drink incident from the previous week. Lets' rock her belief system a bit more, I thought.

I rose, this time without fear of waking her, and went downstairs. Found the Whiskey bottle, and bounded back up the stairs.

'How convenient', I thought, as I saw her mouth gaping wide, and I proceeded to perform the most evil deed I'd ever done in my life. I poured a generous amount of the spirit in her throat. A thought that this action could break her out of her 'coma' didn't enter my head or I might have shit myself at this point. I pulled back the bedclothes, splattered liberal drops of the precious liquid over her 'Night tent' as I called her gown, and a few more on her pillow. Then I stood to admire my handiwork. Now filled with an evil confidence, poured a little more in her mouth, and pushed it shut. Then lifted her heavy arm, placed the now almost empty bottle between her ample breasts, repositioning her arm in a

Midnight on the Dot

loving cuddle, hand wrapped around the neck. Pulled the covers back up, and retreated to the en-suite, suddenly full of fear and trepidation. There I scrubbed my hands as if they were covered in blood, to hide any trace of alcohol, and took some deep breaths to steady myself, before returning to my side of the bed, got in, and waited. I waited for the click, the snort, and the explosion. Doubt entered my head – she'll have me locked up for this. But the deed was done, my fate sealed, I prayed.

An explosive sort of snort nearly made me wet myself, but it quickly subsided into the usually noises, to my great relief. She didn't wake, but did I hear her licking her lips... and the mumbling...let's not go there! Now the bed was rocking rhythmical to the movements of her groin. It painted pictures in my mind which haunt me to this day. Needless to say – I wasn't going to try this again. I thank God for the King size bed, and wish to say no more on the subject of that night.

I was wakened from my nightmare by an ear piercing scream.

My brain, yet again, not finding first gear managed a "Wha..." and a partial sit up, and bleary eye look in Jean's direction. She was never something you could say looked good in the morning, but, boy, did she look bad! All her self belief was stripped away. She looked

Midnight on the Dot

a shadow of her former arrogant, self confident self. She looked vulnerable, and a twinge of guilt surfaced in my mind, mixed with the strange alien thought of how much I actually fancied her in that split second.

"What you looking at" her defence mechanisms clicked into play.

"Arg...You all right?" I offered feebly.

"Why wouldn't I be" she snapped back, the empty Whiskey bottle still clamped to her chest. She was visibly shaken, but her unbreakable belief in the superiority was fighting back. I pointed at the bottle "You've been working too hard, need a break"

Well, I overstepped the mark there, but she couldn't find the words to rebuke me. For the first time since she ensnared me I saw true doubt in her expression, which was quickly turning into venom towards me. Now, I could see her thinking – If she was midnight sleepwalk drinking it was my fault – entirely. "What would you know about hard" she managed, as she leaped from the bed, allowing the bottle to drop to the floor. Did she forget the word work or was thinking of something else I wondered.

That seemed to settle things. She regained her control, she was right, it was my fault. Ok, she was right – but not thanks to the evidence. The rest of the morning

Midnight on the Dot

continued as normal. Except, I was no longer thought of as a burden to weigh her down, hold her back, Now I was her most hated creature in the whole universe.

In a way, for me, it marked an improvement in our relationship. She stopped talking at me almost entirely. If I saw any of her friends while out, before they would whisper to each other and laugh; now they just nodded and glared. Although some of those looks added a touch of desire too... or was that my imagination. What had she told them? Did she know what I did, I don't know. Talking between us was reduced to the absolute minimum, which was fine by me. I was excluded from the marriage bed, another boon, sleeping in the spare room. I slept like a log for the next few weeks. By day, I plotted what I'd do next Dark Hour. I knew it was real now, not a dream, not sleepwalking, but real. I needed to know: how long did it last, did it happen every night, or just when I woke, was it just Jean, or the whole world, and did I wake when it started I had to find out. Staying up passed 11 at night needed an excuse in our household – even if I slept in a different room. An opportunity knocked with a general election, I stating that I would be staying up to watch the results come in. It prompted our first exchange of insults for weeks. I was called a fool (probably the nicest thing she said to me for ages) "It's a foregone conclusion; the right would claim the day". She supported the right, being as she was always right anyway. The left, and myself,

Midnight on the Dot

would always lose. "Maybe for not much longer" was my return, meaning myself more than the left, mostly. Anyway I stayed up, the exit poll proved her right of course "Told you" she shouted from the top of the stairs. "Maybe not, could be wrong" I shouted back, to which she didn't bother to reply as she had the knowledge that she was always right. Of course she was right, but at 12 I still, almost, had hope.

Once she'd gone and her snores could be heard downstairs, I retrieved from its hiding place the hour glass I'd purchased that day. She had not discovered it or I might have to come up with a reason why she shouldn't have me committed there and then. I struggled to stay awake as the tedium of the election count coverage numbed my brain, but with the sudden silence I become alert, turned the hour glass, watched gravity do its work, thankful that it didn't take any time off, and thought what now?

I took a look outside – not raining – good- and stepped out the patio doors. It was a chilly late October night, but I did not feel the cold. The air was still, and the stars were twinkling their hearts out in the clear night sky.

No sound – we lived in suburbia, on the edge of the city, usually you would hear the buzz of the never sleeping metropolis – but no sound. A main road

Midnight on the Dot

passed by the front of the house, a road that never stopped day or night – but no sound. Silence!

I walked round the front of the house to check the road. There were a few cars, but they were not moving, despite being in the carriageways, and occupied by drivers who appeared to be concentrating on the road ahead. I caught sight of a man on the pavement in mid stride just outside my house. I recognised him as a next door neighbour. He had been always complaining about something or other. Jean seemed to take his side in any argument, no matter what. She'd let him borrow my stuff, and then he would only give it back when broken, claiming it was like that when he got it. Jean would, of course, agree, then complain that I shouldn't lend him stuff that didn't work.

I thought I'd take a closer look, to see why he hadn't fallen over. He seemed to be as dead to the world as Jean was, but he was balanced, both feet on the floor – was that luck or do people have the unconscious ability to adjust to the Dark Hour. I touched him ever so lightly just to see if he was fixed to the spot. He wobbled sideways, but stayed upright.

I spied to his side a huge puddle left by an early evening downpour, the gutters being blocked by all the leaves he had blown out of his garden using my blower. So he did still have it, the bastard. It didn't take

Midnight on the Dot

much effort just to tip him over, head first into the dirty water. I'd turned away in glee at my mischief, but realised that the puddle was much deeper than I imagined, his head was nearly swallowed up by the depths. I stood transfixed, should I pull him out a bit? Will he drown? Did I care? Did he deserve such a fate? What about his stuck-up wife and devil spawn kids? Would they care? Probably if the money stopped coming in. Which of course it won't – I'd endured those social evenings where he would pontificate about how well he'd catered for his brood in the "unlikely" event of his death. It's a wonder they hadn't done him in before now, themselves.

I ended my pondering; believing he wouldn't drown anyway. His mouth was still above the muck, and dirty water. How was I to know he was drunk as a lord, and unable to get up?

I thought further of my blower – now was the time to retrieve it. I walked up his drive and down the side of the house. As I passed a window leaking a shaft of light from curtains not fully closed, and I peaked in. They say curiosity killed the cat – for me it just turned my stomach. The room in question was what the neighbour referred to as his games room. That his and the wife's games room, no kids allowed – I always thought he was joking – sorry trying to joke – Boy! Was I wrong. It looked a bit like a torture chamber, lots of chains, whips, leather gear, sharp and strange looking implements the use of which I had no idea - being a total innocent regarding S&M or whatever it's called. But, the thing that caused the upheaval in my gut region, was the sight of herself (the wife -his that is) getting herself ready for the hubbies homecoming. The

Midnight on the Dot

wife was lounging on a sort of bench dressed (I exaggerate) in some leather straps, servicing herself with an oversized vibrator. Now that lady clothed was of a shape and size only another Hippo could love (In my book – but each to his own, as they say) The expression on her face was frightening, that's all I'm prepared to say at this juncture, let's leave it there. The man in the puddle was of a slight build; his wife could easily crush him to death with all that gear.

I pulled myself away from the chamber of horrors, and run back to my house. As I passed the prone deviant in the pool, I gave him a hard kick in the privates, to spoil his fun so I thought, and raced back inside.

One look at the hour glass told me I'd used up half an hour of the Dark Time – I didn't yet know if I could call it an hour.

I decided it would be prudent to wait the rest out, so I sat and waited. I nodded off a couple of times with only an ugly lying, gloating, face staring back from the TV, but lost only seconds. I watched the sand grains fall. Nearer and nearer it got to the bottom, and as the last grain fell I was startled out of reverie by the politician finishing his lie. The volume seemed very loud, until my brain got used to the return of sound.

Enough, I turned off the TV, re-hid the timer, and went up to bed, and fell fitfully asleep.

I was shaken out of my dreams by Jean shaking me violently.

"Wake up, you dolt, wake up, police!"

"What" again my reactions where perfectly innocent thanks to brain in park mode. "Police...what?"

"At the door, asking if you saw anything in the street around twelve or so, you where up, I told them so!"

Midnight on the Dot

"What time is it now?"
"It's 2 o'clock, now get up and get rid of them".
I arose, and gingerly went down stairs, thinking – the neighbours complained I pushed him over?
"Em, I'm sorry to bother you Mr Wyrd, did you happen to see or hear anything from the street at around 1am, I understand you were up at that time, sir".
"Arrr, no, was watching the election count in the back room, falling asleep really, saw the clock hit 12 and crawled off to the spare room, again at the back of the house...To not disturb the wife...light sleeper... Why what's happened?" I feigned only partial interest.
"Oh! Bit bazaar really" It was a young, rookie cop standing at the door.
"Guy drowned in a puddle by his wife dressed in S&M gear, bit disgusting really, she's built like a hippo, we arrived to see her shaking him up a down, screaming "How dare you. Die now" we think, you didn't hear that, no? Your wife heard the "Die now" bit".
"No, heard nothing, sorry".
"Sorry for bothering you Sir, have a good night" and with that he left.

Jean was called as witness in the trial, the dead man's wife claims she just found him lying there head underwater, and was trying to resuscitate him.
Nobody believed her, when the insurance policies came to light. Of course I could hardly leap in and say she was innocent, and claim it was an accident. No one would believe me. When her costume was produced, innocence was not something she could claim, if you know what I mean. The whole neighbourhood was talking of her shame.

Midnight on the Dot

Her husband's death unhinged her, so she would have ended up confined to a mental institution, anyway, but may be not a penal one, so I didn't dwell too long on my guilt. I did realise that I needed to be a bit more careful in future, or this new found opportunity will claim me.

What of their kids, the devil spawn, you ask? Well, they were taken off by the government and put into an institution that specialised in training up kids to be hardened criminals. I had been convinced that was where those brutes were heading anyway, so no real harm done, but I never got my blower back. Evidence the cops said... bastards.

To Jean, it was my entire fault she was woken from her beauty sleep. I held my tongue – regarding the last bit. Anyway I decided it would be prudent not to use the Dark Hour (As I can now safely call it) for a while until the trial was done and dusted. Added to that, I had no idea what to do with it. I needed an opportunity when she was up past midnight and I could arrange an alibi, if I was ever to get shot of her. So I bided my time.

My opportunity approached when Jean forewarned me of her impending Christmas 'Coven' party, with all baggage (Meaning husbands) brought along for their pleasure (Not ours, Oh no. The witches pleasure of showing off the burdens, to boast that this is why their lives are such a trial – Martyrs – all of them). I considered it nothing short of a nightmare. I had a suspicion about the timing of these events, Halloween had only just past, with Christmas still weeks away, why not be honest and hold it on All Hollows Eve, but then they were probably all too busy riding around on their broomsticks. But it's not the ladies themselves

Midnight on the Dot

that bug me most about these nights. No, it's the husbands themselves – a bunch of feeble minded bores, and I would be expected to go and play nicely with the 'boys' in a separate room while the witches hogged the booze, and the food in the kitchen , discussing our (the husbands) limitations. It was one of the few times a year Jean was happy to stay up late, the longer she could drag out the horror the happier she was. She even thought she was doing me a favour by being allowed to play with the 'Boys'. I was told, very definitely to not upset the host's husband this time, and not to drink too much, and she'd be watching me like a hawk. Oh what joy!
Most of the 'Boys' were Civil Servants of the most boring type. They all seem to have bazaar hobbies to make their lives bearable for themselves but unbearable for those who didn't share their love. Two of the guys raced old Jags. Now that, you would think would make them interesting people to talk to, but no. Last year I endured a half hour or more discussion on Jaguar radiator grills from 1947 to 1949 or some other years, who knows, who cares. Mind numbed, I left to find another drink, by the time I got back the two were still on the same subject, but the exchange had become heated, and others were stepping in to separate them. Their wives were summoned to take their 'boys' home and the party broke up. In the car on route back home, Jean said "What did you say to upset them?" So it was my fault for ending her fun.
For this year's 'do' I was warned and given 'the look'. It was best behaviour or...or... my life would get worse? Is that even possible I thought. The 'Dark Hour' better happen this time. What am I saying – the whole night

Midnight on the Dot

was the Dark Hour where time moved like treacle – was that how it started. My mind reached a point so dark and deep that I magicked the Dark Hour?... What bollocks.
The offending date with utter boredom and humiliation arrived; I was suited, booted, and scrubbed so clean I gleamed. Jean tut-tutted, but accepted that I could not be improved upon, and off we went. Our destination was only 5 minutes walk, but we got a cab anyway. On arrival, I was presented to the coven. I got the usual collection of disdainful looks, plus a couple of 'I'm slightly interested if you fancy giving me some fun' looks, and pure hate from the rest. That is, except for one woman I'd never seen before. She did not have the same confident look as the others... new girl... brought in probably to get her husband in bed. They always seem to find one every year. Most newbie's never graduate to full grown bitch, and this one looked totally lost. She was giving me a strange look, and turned away with a guilty look as soon as our eyes met. Oooh! I might be in there, my dirty mind thought, roll on midnight. Three hours to the hour, this is going to be the longest evening ever.
Once the usual unpleasantness's had been exhausted, I was sent off with my 'lunch box and drink' (one plain ham sandwich and a beer) to play with the 'boys' in the games room. Out of the frying pan into oblivion.
Like with the girls, we, the boys, had a newbe too. The new girl's husband, obviously, was holding court, so it seems. He was handsome (not to me I stress) in an ugly way, tallish, thanks to platform soles, and a full head of fake hair. He was well bronzed (from a bottle I would say) He was brash, loud, confident, and a

Midnight on the Dot

fountain of bullshit
Normally my entrance would be greeted by a level of apathy, along with a few 'Oh God, not him' looks. Most of the boys didn't realise how boring they were, but this time I was greeted by a few hopeful looks, looks that pleaded with me to shut his guy up.
I failed. Gerald, as he was called, was not a listener. He talked nonstop, cracked mirthless, tasteless jokes, found ways to offend everyone in the room, except me. I'm not saying I'm not a wimp, just saying I gave up giving a shit what anybody says about, or at, me a long time ago. I must say, it was the first time at one of these do's that the others looked as bored and annoyed as I was.

I started to enjoy their discomfort, serves them right, the boring, brain-dead, old farts. Then the noise stopped mid sentence, and all was still. I breathed a sigh of relief and wondered how I could make him suffer. I was standing far too close to him, if I did anything, I would get the blame, *'bugger'* I thought *'should have been watching the time'*. I was caught in indecision when the door to the room burst open and a totally naked woman bearing two long carving knives bounded in. I believe we both screamed in surprise – I managed to knock into Gerald, who in turn brought every one of "the boys" down with him, like nine pins.

The clatter of falling 'statues' wrested my attention from the naked apparition.

Midnight on the Dot

"Shit" I spluttered, then remembered the knives, and snapped back in their direction.

"Strike" I heard, followed by a giggle and then a burst of sobbing. The apparition was now only partly visible, trying to hide behind a large coffee table.

"You're naked?" It wasn't the question I was looking for.

"You see me?" wasn't the reply I expected, either. I had not expected any reply, thinking for a moment, I was dreaming again.

The sobbing stopped as quickly as it started. "Bollocks, can't get anything right with this one" said the nudist. At that point I saw her face. It was the newbie, wife to Gerald. I remembered her name.

"Kate – that you, you see the dark hour too" I still wasn't getting to the question I wanted answering.

"Suppose so, if that's what it's called" said the curled up ball behind the coffee table.

"The knives?" Now I was getting closer to what I needed to know.

"Oh you noticed"

"Just about"

Midnight on the Dot

"Oh shit...You met my husband?"

"Gerald?"

"Yes....were they..Meant for him?" I hoped.

"Yes, you see what he's like, makes my life a misery. I'm not allowed friends, he gets violently jealous if another man even looks in my direction – accuses me of encouraging them. He hits me, I so wanted him dead."

"But naked?"

"So I don't get blood on my clothes. I just go to the bathroom and wash myself off, get dressed, return to the ladies and have an alibi."

"But we won't have?" At this point I noticed a photo on the floor. It had dropped from her mouth where she had carried in, it seemed to show two naked bodies entwined in a 'friendly' embrace. A birth mark on the plentiful arse of the one I can only describe as female was very familiar. The other had a mop of uncontrollable blond hair very similar to the Gerald currently lying on the floor, in a compromising position with one of the 'other' boys.

I pointed at the picture and managed 'Wha...'

Midnight on the Dot

The would be murderer raised her head, bit her lip and then said "Gerald...and your wife... I was going to put it in your pocket after I'd ..." she made stabbing motions with both hands still clutching those wicked looking knives.

"And place my hand on the blades – for fingerprints, I accused."

She nodded "Sorry..." she offered, with a worried look on her face.

"Don't blame you really I suppose. I was also prepared to kill him myself – he's welcome to the wife, by the way."

"Oh, I don't think I could do it anyway – I had chickened the moment I saw him."

"Do you still love him?"

"No – fuck off – he's a bloody bastard"

There followed a brief period of silence as we both tried to come to adjust to this new reality.

"Em.... I think you ought to get dressed....you know......before the hour is up...Will you turn away?...please."

"Em" Was all I could manage while staring at the knives still within her hands. *'What the hell, you only*

Midnight on the Dot

live once', and I turned, wondering why I thought that. I heard the door close as I gazed at the mess before me.

Then shock set in, I was staring at one spot amongst the fallen bodies when the fully clothed Kate came back in. "I spiked all their drinks" She stopped "Shit!"

We both stared at the spreading blood stain on the beige carpet. It was a lot of blood. Kate and myself approached the pile of bodies tentatively then she took a sharp intake of breath, at the same time I noticed blood on the corner of a heavy and ugly side table.

I heard her give a little chuckle which drew my attention to the back of Gerald's head – the source of the pool of blood.

"Oh my God" she said with an edge of delight, "is he dead, do you think" She looked at me with an expression of a child asking if Santa's coming.

"Not yet, possibly...but by the time he wakes he will be"

"What"

"Em....he's losing blood at quite a rate – even if his injury is not fatal, the blood loss will kill him. I have no idea how we can stop it"

"Stop it! Why would we stop it" she snapped

Midnight on the Dot

"Ah...oh well I Am going to get the blame for this. I know that's what you planned...isn't it"

"Yes – but that was before"

"Before what?"

"You see the Dark hour, I Am not alone"

"Oh yes"

"And you saw me naked"

"Mmm, nice it was too" I mused aloud, and went red.

"So you owe me".

"Ah, you owe me surely. I've done your job for you".

"Oh that...No you have to give me a peek".

"Hang on, we got bodies and blood all over the place and you're thinking of... Sex?"

"No..not sex...at least not until I've seen it..you know" She made shapes with her fingers indicating length and girth.

"Can we just sort out the business in hand" I said whilst feeling an involuntary stirring of my loins. She giggled, obviously thinking of my 'business' in her hands. I grew a little more...red faced.

Midnight on the Dot

"Fuck me woman!" I regretted saying that immediately. Her grin broadened.

"Chill John, just go to the toilet in the hall till the end of the hour, and come out when you hear the screams. You'll be in the clear then."

"But the witches... won't have seen me leave this room, and the men will believe I was in here at the time."

"Anybody having to suffer my hus...'Ex's diatribe for more than ten minutes will have probably forgotten who they are, let alone who was in the room with them. And those bitches are too much up their own arses to notice your movements, just make an entrance when you come out."

A short silence followed, in which Kate's logic burned through into my brain cells. I nodded.

"How much time do we have left?" I asked.

She produced an hour glass from her bag, showing that only a third of our time was gone.

"Plenty!" she said with an expression on a face that meant what she proved to me she meant.

Midnight on the Dot

With 5 minutes left of the hour we both dressed again, and Kate left the toilet to retake her position in the kitchen, and I waited for the commotion to start.

And there was one... Shouts and screams, and the sound of panic. I flushed the cistern, and made my entrance to the throng.

Kate was already in floods of tears. One of the 'boys' had burst from the 'games room' covered in blood shouting "Gerald's dead". There followed a period of general confusion, shouting, accusation, denials and general puzzlement. The cops were finally called. I was largely ignored while Kate with her false tears was being comforted. Jean looked at me, with the look meaning 'What did you do?'

It was suggested by someone that Gerald had upset Fred, the man he bled on and were having a row, I went along with it adding a suspicion that Gerald was doing the dirty with one, or more, of the wives. Fred's wife, Gladys, having drunk far more vino than was sensible, started verbally abusing him for being useless between the sheets, and what was a girl in her prime supposed to do. It was probably only wishful thinking, but it was reinforced by the rest of the ladies leaping in to defend her husband, thus freeing themselves from suspicion of wrong doing. Fred's denials fell upon deaf ears. The cops were satisfied,

Midnight on the Dot

and I was off the hook. Did I feel guilt about Fred's fate...Well not when it was deemed accidental, and no charges brought. Added to that Gladys, it seems looked upon her husband in a new light, he was now her hero, defending her honour. He was a new man, a killer, a man to be feared, no longer pre-occupied with radiator grills, started driving his vintage Jag like a maniac, with his loving wife beside him for the trills. I didn't get to their funeral, Oh well.

Anyway, the evening ended in tears all round. Except for myself....and Jean. She may have been shagging Gerald, but it didn't mean she actually liked the man. One of the 'boys' gave Kate an escort home, came back with a red cheek, I stayed clear of trouble. When we were finally allowed to go Jean remained silent for all the 5 minutes home. When inside she looked as if she was going to question me but she just shook her head and stormed off to bed.

Once in bed, myself, I finally got to think about the evenings events. What a turn up – someone else experienced the Dark hour. A patient of my wife, while my beloved was banging the her patients husband, who ends up dead. I have sex in a toilet with a would be 'axe' murderer.... Interesting night...or what?

Midnight on the Dot

I didn't get much sleep that night. In the morning Jean looked as if she had been crying all night. WTF – did she love him! Surely not!!

"You alright love" I lied, then bit my tongue.

"Why shouldn't I be" she snapped

"Trauma filled night" I offered

"Hmm – not that you care"

"What do you mean – a man died – I might not have liked the bore but – he died" I didn't know what I was trying to say. There was no more conversation that day.

The following night I was woken by a loud knocking at the front door. I looked at the clock cursing whoever was making that racket, midnight on the dot...'Oh'

I raced downstairs, peaked through the spy hole to see Kate, undressed for action. I opened the door on her nakedness. "Wha.." I managed.

"Come on we've got half an hour" she enthused.

"For what?" I spluttered. .'Was I dim or what' was I expression she gave back. "Oh" I added as the obvious dawned on me.

Midnight on the Dot

She bounded up to Jean's bedroom with me trailing in her wake. I was becoming concerned she hadn't meant what I'd first thought she meant...but she did – in Jean's bed...With Jean lying there. WTF – I convinced her that I thought that it was a bit off putting so we went into the spare bedroom instead.

I wanted to talk, but she wanted passion, I obliged. Then as quick as she appeared she was gone, with the words "my place tomorrow, come naked"., and I did, several times. This back and forth continued for several weeks. I had become unable to fall asleep before 12 since the party.

There wasn't much conversation in those meetings and I had so much to say, or ask, or something. Then one night she came to my place fully clothed ... "Need to talk" she said – I agreed.

"Your wife has gotta go, she suspects something" It seems Kate was still attending Jean as a patient.

"She's not said anything to me at all, but does give me a strange look now and again".

"She's got to go" she repeated.

"How, she's rarely out of bed at midnight"

"Midnight Mass Christmas Eve"

Midnight on the Dot

"In church, you want to kill her in church"

"Who said anything about me; you're the one with the deadly touch"

"Whoa – they were accidents – I'm not a killer – you're the one bursting in with carrying knives to kill your husband"

"But I couldn't go through with it...accidents?...more than one?"

"Look – I'm expected to sit with her through the whole bloody.......... nightmare – how can I do it and get away with it"

"So you're not going to do it"

"I didn't say that, the timing has got to be right, I need to be elsewhere when it happens...for an alibi"

"You won't do it will you – you're a coward John"

"Hang on, I want her gone just as much as you, but this has got to be right – OK"   She was silent for a while.

"OK but don't leave it too long John – she knows something"

"She knows nothing, though she suspects everything, different thing entirely"

Midnight on the Dot

"Ok John, have it your way... anyway, back to normal tomorrow night, my place, and do come naked, saves time..." She kissed me passionately, and left.

I had hoped for a break, to be totally honest. I was getting tired of these midnight jaunts. Don't get me wrong, I loved the sex, but the waiting for midnight was losing its novelty, but I was hooked.

So, on the dot of Midnight the following night, I stripped off my clothes as requested and ran naked through the streets the short distance to her house. The thrill of the night air tingling my nether regions had worn off too. I cursed her when I found she had not left the front door open. Instead, she had stuck a tiny post-it note on the front door which said "Back door open, please remove note" *'bitch'* I thought, she was starting playing games now. The route to the back door meandered its way through some overgrown and unforgiving bushes. I had no torch with me (obviously) and it was a moonless night. The bitch was really annoying me now, had half a mind to not 'fuck her' and return home, but...

I made it the kitchen door with remarkably few scrapes, and minor bleeds, but that did not reduce my desire to punish her the way she liked...bitch. To my disappointment she was not waiting on the kitchen table, or on the rug in the lounge, nor on the dining

Midnight on the Dot

table, nor in the broom cupboard (to my relief, could never understand what she liked about that one), and I exhausted all the places to look down stairs. I was getting fed up with her games; she was getting worse with them. I shouted upstairs, but the bitch was silent, no clues then, this was getting beyond a joke. I bounded up the stairs, and searched, but found no sign of her, now I was getting angry – what's she playing at?

Downstairs again I went, and there, in the hall, on the inside of the front door was another tiny post-it. Scrawled in tiny writing it said "Sorry John, got call, Fathers dying, too late to cancel, must fly. Will call. Sorry, Kate".

WTF! I cursed her again, never even knew she had a Father. I left by the front door and now feeling a little embarrassed by my nakedness, trudged home staying out of the lamp light. Once home, I went straight up to bed, where I eventually fell asleep dreaming of chasing Kate through the streets of the town, in daylight, whilst I'm naked, and she teasing me with my clothes. Bitch!.

Next thing I knew, the alarm was screaming at me to rise.

"Bollocks" I shouted, then regretted, Jean would be bound to comment upon my swearing.

Midnight on the Dot

But silence greeted my outburst. I listened, no thundering around, no off key opera singing, just silence.

What day is this, surely it's a work day – checked the clock – yes it is, it's not like her to sleep in. I rose from my bed in the spare room, on the landing the bathroom door was wide open – so not in there. I approach her bedroom door with trepidation – it was still closed. I open the door with a smidgen of trepidation, but I was not prepared for what I saw. Jean had been turned into a pin cushion, with every sharp knife we possessed driven into her body. There was no expression on her face, this could only have happened in the Dark Hour. There was blood everywhere.

I suppose I should have realised that Kate planned this all along, and I played her game. If only I'd known about her previous husbands, the ones before Gerald all murdered on the dot of midnight. Coincidence?

Jean was her shrink, she probably knew about the others...possibly.

Why did I call the cops, there and then - that I'll never understand? They found my discarded blood stained clothes in a bin three houses down. She must have worn them to do the deed while I run naked about the town.

Midnight on the Dot

Well that's my story, I swear it's true.

Signed   Rick wyrd

****

John Forbes put down the confession.

"Look Rick... as your lawyer, I got to tell you that as a defence against the murder of your wife, this is....useless...counter-productive...

Confessing to the involvement in two possibly preventable deaths, that you were never in the frame for, hardly helps your case. Claiming that Kate, the D.A.s future wife I might add, is a serial husband killer, that poor unfortunate woman, won't help you one bit... Your best bet is a plea of insanity, at least this will give fuel to that claim. The "Dark Hour" for heaven's sake... Still it could save you from death row... and you never know, you could even sell it as a short story, maybe it will pay for my bill!"

*****

Prologue:

The sanatorium isn't such a bad place, once you get used to my screams. I don't wake at midnight, on the dot, anymore – possibly due to the drugs.

Midnight on the Dot

Kate popped in to see me one night, I presume. I was lucky; a passing guard cut me down, and resuscitated me, before I was a goner. They didn't believe me as to how I came by the length rope in my cell. They upped my drugs after that, making it so... hard...keep wri......

Begrudgery

I gotta tell you
That your art work's not worth a light.
Your self-portrait looks like it's been in a fight.
Just because they've hung you up in the Tate.
Me. I'd just burn 'em. Would'nt..... Hesitate.

I gotta tell you
Your poems really, really, really stink.
That's the truth, not just wot I fink.
The fact they made you a lau-re-ate;
You can't even rhyme, so you're crap, anyway.

I gotta tell you
Your songs are a load a shit.
If I were you I'd really want to quit.
The fact you got golden discs, Grammies by the ton,
Doesn't really mean you appeal to anyone.

I gotta tell you
Your latest book really kind a sucks;
Just 'cause it's earned few million bucks,
And been serialised, and sold the film rights.
Still, it's only good for wiping my arse when I get the shites.

I gotta tell you
I know you're a talentless bum.
All the accolades and trophies you won
Count for nothing. You're no better than me;
It's only recently your family fell out the tree.

I gotta tell you
Your fame should belong to me.
It's an injustice – why can you not see?
The fact I'm useless, and lazy as could be,
Will never ever stop my begrudgery.

If Only

If Only

If only I had turned to the right?

If only!...My life would have been oh so different.

I would not be lying here surrounded by the debris of yesterday's binge drinking session, still drunk, or whatever, soiled, dishevelled, unshaven, and naked. If I had turned to the right on leaving the flat that day, I would have caught that bus, got to that interview, got the job (it was nailed on I was told), kept the flat, got the girl, got the house, got the family, eventually retiring on a 'comfortable' pension.

But no! I just had to go and turn to the left!

What's the difference you might ask?

The bus stops an equidistance in either direction from that flat, right or left, though it leaves the right-side one 2 minutes earlier.

So what was so bad about turning left?

Well...I'll tell you – Public Houses!... No pubs to the right...well, none that I had not been banned from. To the left there's still one landlord who would not throw me out on sight, mainly because I never go in that one by choice – bloody rip-off merchant, he is...

If Only

Now I got you thinking – he's a bloody alcoholic – can't pass by a drinking hole without going in for a drink, what chance would he ever have of holding down a job, relationship, marriage, etc. – ah none you say!

Well you are wrong, I had turned over a new leaf, drying out, getting that job, and I was not going into a pub to get a drink, so there.

So what was the problem with going past a pub?

I blame the coffee!

Look, I was not used to getting up before midday before that day, needed four large mugs of caffeine to wake me up. Then there was the state of my bathroom... My first pay check would pay to fix the toilet. So when I left the place I needed to pay a visit, so to speak.

Now, to the right there was a public loo, but there was no way I was going in there in my interview suit. I would come out of that hole, stinking like an incontinent tramp, and the bus driver would throw me off the bus. Then, of course, I had run-ins with the local low-life's who frequent that den of iniquity – me in a suit – red rag to a bull – I'll say no more on that.

So left I went, and entered the one pub I could still go in, and was immediately confronted by the landlord of the establishment who issued unto me a question I

If Only

could only answer one way, even then, in spite of my resolution.

"What will you be having sir" the bastard asked.

Now, I may have been considering the wagon and climbing aboard but on this occasion I only had one stock answer, me being more concerned regarding avoiding the soiling of my trousers, at that moment.

"Pint of best." There I said it – shit...well I didn't, but went to relieve myself, hoping he did not hear me. On my return to the bar area a foaming pint of what this landlord considered 'Best' stood on the counter alongside his outstretched hand looking for payment . *'Bugger'* me thinks, *'Oh well – one will be alright'* and it was, in case you're thinking otherwise. Another thought I had was : now I would not have enough money to buy a sandwich. *'Double bugger'*.

I downed the pint with ease, thanked the bar-lord for condemning me to starvation, and left the pub, also with ease, but in my rush to remove myself from further temptation I had left my change on the bar counter. I was another 20 yards down the road when this fact dawned on me. Quandary – no money for the bus if I carry on, or possibility of missing my bus if I return for the dosh. Not really a quandary I resolved – without the money – thrown off the bus. I vowed to return post haste to the pub, snatch my change from the bar and

If Only

leg it before the Bar man could say a word, and run to the bus.

It was at that moment that I saw it. It was on the ground, to my left – for left was, again, the direction I spun in my effort to regain my cash – had I turned to my right I would never have seen it, I would have completed my task, got bus, attended that interview, got the job, etc, etc. But No I turned that fateful left – again.

What, you ask impatiently, was the thing that made me miss my bus, and the opportunities that mode of transport was offering.

Well, it was a brand spanking new and unused 50 smackers note just lying there, unsullied, unattended, unloved, forgotten, and waiting... for me.

I should say that it was not that notes fault that I missed my bus; I take full responsibility of that, before you start accusing.

I froze in mid spin, quickly glanced up and down the street to make sure I could see no possible former owner of the afore mentioned fifty. I determined that it must have been discarded casually by someone nowhere near as needy as myself, a donation to me in other words. Another quick glance up and down the street, to make doubly sure no one could see me pick

If Only

it up... a fifty note could get you mugged you know. But the street was deserted. I snatched it up pronto; it was mine, my precious...

Did I then lope off at a steady gallop to the bus stop?

No!

Why?

Because the bus driver would never allow me on without the correct change – and there was no way I was going to say "keep it".

A few yards further on there was an open-all-hours corner shop, so I nipped in to ask the counter person to change the note. The local foreign gentleman ensconced at the till looked mystified; he didn't seem to understand a single word I said (My London accent see – been down south a lot). After a few valuable minutes of gesticulation and sign language I gave up and bought something, getting change from the fifty, and left.

But I turned to the right... Back the way I came. '*Bugger*' I thought as I found myself back outside the pub containing my hard unearned cash.

'*Sod it*' I thought, '*not letting that greedy bastard have my money*', and so in I went. There was my cash still where I left it, and there was the ever present bar-lord.

If Only

"Same again" he said – quick as a flash.

'*Bastard*' I thought... "Yep" I vocally reflexed.

I had no defence against his statement – because it was a statement where I was concerned, not a question. My fate was now sealed. The pint downed, my bladder I emptied again, while the barman took the liberty of filling my glass again – there was no escape... For me.

The filling and emptying continued a pace, until the landlord claimed the entire cash was spent. An argument ensued as to the accuracy of his claim, which ended with myself lying face down in the gutter outside the pub, while being told to "never darken my door step again".

Needless to say, I never got the bus, job, girl, house etc. after that.

So all because I turned left, instead of right, I now lay here in a jobless semi-drunken stupor.

If only I'd turn right, I would have got that bus, got abuse from the regular bus passengers seeing me in a suit, got to that interview, got that stinking lousy job, kept my shit hole of a flat, got hooked by that shag-bag 'Lazy' Daisy (she being up the duff and claimed the sprog was mine, if I had money) got mortgaged to the hilt, got puked on by screaming kids, got divorced, got

If Only

into negative equity, and end up being found dead face down in my own vomit. Probably!

Instead I lie here, on my own sun drenched pacific island, waited on hand and, and, everywhere in fact, surrounded by lovely young and very friendly girls, with not a care in the world.

What? You say – How come?

Well, it's thanks to that Euro Millions lottery ticket I bought in the corner shop to get change for that 50.

Word of advice chaps – never ever turn right.

If Only.

Hello, what's this you ask... It's not a continuation of 'If Only'. No this is something else, but it's not in the contents?

An explanation:

Since I have dabbled in the music arena in a small way (extremely small) I have decided to introduce to the literary scene something which was (maybe still is) popular in some genres of the music fraternity not that long ago – The Hidden Track... a piece of whatever that the band wouldn't normally issue on an album. A Freebee for the fans, so to speak. A testing of the waters maybe.

Well here's my hidden track. No title, no further explanation. Something a little different.

Over the past months I have seen, read and researched a number of conspiracy theories posted on the interwebby thingy claiming that Covid-19 was purposely created and spread by man.

I have NOT been particularly impressed, so far, with their offerings.

So I've decided to knock up my own one. Evidence Based!

If this pandemic was purposefully kicked off then that would be a crime, and we should look for evidence like in the TV progs : motive, means, and opportunity. The latter two would be anybody with access to a lab, and knowledge about viruses, or money/power over those who do. I'll leave them there.

Now motive: Let's leave out madness, stupidity, or for the fun of it, you would go mad yourself trying to make sense of that. No, let us presume who ever did it was clever enough to have an end game and a clear objective, and the ability to achieve it.

If money was the motive then where is the ransom note? If you planned to cover the world with a plague and wanted to profit by it, common sense would suggest, you would already have the antidote, and you would be an idiot to wait till every country in the world spends millions on research for the cure and have any number of "promising" vaccines in testing, before stepping up and saying "and here's one I made earlier, pay up now".

Oh, that anti-malaria drug (starts with H and has a lot of letters) don't count, cause if The Trump is using it nobody with half a brain cell should think it works (and I've seen no scientific research that proves that Trump is actually human).Don't go quoting from those "America's Frontline Doctors" propaganda. The Tea Party Patriots had to scrape the barrel to come up with that lot. Half of them looked so embarrassed to be wearing their monogrammed white coats the political group gave them to wear. I found no evidence that any of them got anywhere near the Covid frontline – 2 Eye Docs(One gave up practice after 4 years) 2 paediatricians (kid doctors – sorry I can't spell) one of whom made the claim that she hasn't lost a patient – I should bloody well hope so - she works in a shopping mall clinic with kids – no idea if she's ever seen someone with Coronavirus, and I won't give space to the stuff she's claimed – total nutcase in my opinion for what it's worth.

Anyway –enough of that tripe – on with my 'show and tell'.

If the moneys from another source it would have to be for something the perpetrator had sole rights to, otherwise they would be risking losing to competitors.

No. It all seems a bit risky... and 'Big-business' don't like risky – sure things are what they back, no three-legged donkeys hoping that all the horses drop dead.

I should add that in all good detective shows (and the bad ones) when a rich man is accused of doing a crime for money, all he has to say is "But I'm rich, I don't need the money" and he ceases to be a suspect.

You have to remember that no one could have predicted how things would go – as it is there is little consistency in how each country has tackled the pandemic, and now it's getting even more random.

So, for me, money as a motive would be a gamble only someone mad or stupid and I said I'm ignoring them.

Power – is that a motive. My feeling on that puts me back to mad or stupid, I'm thinking. I know you conspiracy theorists seem to think there is some overriding controlling force or organisation 'up there' manipulating us all, but I don't. I'm not saying nobody is trying to control us, just that they are making an awful job of it.

What we need is evidence:

Is there a cure already out there, maybe there is!

Over the last few weeks I've come across a number of pieces of research by scientists, doctors, etc. which though lacking peer review currently, or the opportunity to carry out large scale testing (which of course means they are perfect for use in a conspiracy theory) (but since I haven't twisted the conclusions of the authors to fit my ethos – maybe...just maybe?...)

1) Eating plenty of fruit and vegetables seems to help people avoid catching the virus.
2) In Canada it has been claimed that the consumption of CBD Oil/Weed also reduces the likelihood of succumbing.
3) In Italy Doctors have claimed noticing that men with a full head of hair make up a much smaller proportion of male ICU patients than those in the general population (Ok – they said bald blokes fare worse – just trying to be positive)
4) A good dose of vitamin D helps it seems (At least , a deficiency in that area makes matters worse)
5) The virus spreads more vigorously indoors.

The last two would suggest outdoor living would be a good idea

Any pattern yet, you think?

What about actual effects so far?

Where have the biggest clusters of Covid-19 infections been found?

1) Competitive sports events (Cheltenham, Football matches, etc) Competitive people put on hold.
2) Old Folks homes (containing the last generation of people in which the majority thought major Wars could be justified) "Peace Man"
3) Meat processing plants? What's that about? Could be a shortage of meat! Why not offices where no real cleaning precautions (Don't get me started about office cleaning – I spent 50 years working in filthy offices in the private sector surrounded by streaming colds and flu's) Surely the meat industry took precautions?

Other effects:
1) The City rat race closed – Life slows down...Chill Man!
2) A drop in pollution. Clean air and clean waters.
3) Air Flights to "exotic" places ended – those places become exotic again.
4) People being paid not to work.
5) Plants and wildlife bouncing back.
6) Hairdressers and barbers shut – grief to those who like short hair.

Can you see it yet?

Well I think it's bloody obvious!

It's the Militant Vegan Hippy wing of the Green Party.

Finally – something you can really blame them for.

Oh before you accuse me of some insider knowledge – me with my long hair and weird musical tastes, and an aversion to red meat and some dairy products, I claim the reverse Clinton defence
    I never smoked...But I did inhale.!

The End.

Backward

No animals were harmed during the making of this book. The goat molestation in "Why Me" was merely alleged. There's no proof...OK.

And don't believed a word that lab rat says!

Note: The diagram at the front of "The Pact" was not produced to help you understand what is going on. I did it to show how confused I got while trying to write it (Believe it or not – it's an EXEL spreadsheet. I kid you not)

Only one...or maybe two items within this tome are in anyway autobiographical. There's a prize of a bullet through the head for anyone who can guess which ones.

If you have any complaints - go to your doctor, don't trouble me with them. Alternatively you can Email me via Buzzzwyrd@gmail.com , I could do with a laugh.

Really the End

About the Author:

An English exile from east of London who moved to Wexford loads of years ago. After several successful careers of a technical nature, he inexplicably ended up a member of the Irish Civil Service. During this period of what he loosely refers employment (or 'Semi-retirement' - It was his brain that was fully retired) he took to writing stuff and nonsense to combat madness and utter boredom (unsuccessfully according to some). He ventured into verse and song writing of a humorous nature, Examples of the results can be found in the Webbything on SOUNDCLOUD under the name Buzzzwyrd, aided and abetted by the talented Mr Buzzz, James McIntyre (The author himself being the Wyrd part of the duo)

Since fully retiring he has turned his attention to staying bed longer, drinking more, and writing short stories (he gets bored quickly) this tome being a random collection of some of them.

He is a member of the South Wexford Writers club, and is in hiding in Rosslare Strand. (He claims to not be a poet, nor an artist, and the evidence is contained within.)

Vol II is in the pipeline for early 2021.

The Complete and Final End.

Now piss off you lot, ain't you got no homes to go to

Oh I dream to hear that refrain again!

Good Day to you all.

Printed in Poland
by Amazon Fulfillment
Poland Sp. z o.o., Wrocław